Name-a-Meen
WIN

Hey, naming a seriously scary meenmaach from Syntilla. It has a glowing antenna-type thing on top of its head, which emits a 'shock'. The vicious creatures hunt in packs, and if they touch you with their antennae five or six times, you lose consciousness. THAT's when they begin to eat you with those razor-sharp teeth – from the toes up! The name had to be not more than 12 letters, and a combination of words from two Indian languages, or from an Indian language and English.

THE WINNING NAME FOR THE MEENMAACH:

BIJLIMAACH

AND THE MOST MASTASTIC MEENMAACH NAMER:

Ankur Chattopadhyay, 13, Kerala Samajam Model School, Jamshedpur

***

THE WINNERS IN OTHER CATEGORIES!

Most Fun:

SHOKHEERA: Like Shakira! Shock + Heera (diamond in Hindi)) – Urvish Paresh Mehta, 16, St Francis D'Assisi High School, Mumbai

Most Number of Entries:

27! Of which we liked **GLOSHAWK** the best – Sara Karthik, 11, Vidya Mandir Senior Secondary School, Chennai

Also Shudder-worthy: *From earthkins:*

* CHAMAK-SLICER – Tarang Shah, 11, Inventure Academy, Bangalore
* PIRANGLER: Cross between a piranha and an angler fish – Arnav Sinha Roy, 13, Meadows International School, Dubai
* EIVILLISH – Maanasa Srikanth, 9, Bangalore
* KHAUF KHATRAL – Aishwarya Ramanath, 12, National Academy for Learning, Bangalore
* BIJLORNE: Bijli ('electricity' in Hindi) + Horn, meaning creature with an electric-powered horn – Vaishnavi D., 16, G.K. Shetty Vivekananda Vidyalaya Junior College, Chennai
* JHATKALEECH – Sanjana Rao, 10, The International School, Bangalore
* PUKKAKADI: Pukka ('absolute' in Hindi) + Kadi ('bite' in Tamil) – Rasika Bharadwaj, 10, Aldenham School, Hertfordshire, UK
* GHATAKMEEN: Lethal Fish – Shagun Vinay Kishan, 11, Indus International School, Bangalore

Most mastastic entry from an older earthkos:

* VIDYUTAXIHU: Vidyut (Sanskrit or Hindi for 'electricity') + Xihu (Assamese for 'river dolphin') – Siddhartha Sarma, 29, Delhi

We hope you succeed in staying right out of the way of the bijlimaach, and enjoy our mastastic fifth adventure too!

TARANAUTS ZARPA, ZVALA AND TUFAN

* THE MOST MASTASTIC MEENMAACH NAMER GETS BOOKS WORTH RS 1500 + TARANAUTS SUPERSTUFF FROM HACHETTE INDIA * ALL WINNERS GET A GIFT HAMPER FROM HACHETTE INDIA + TARANAUTS SUPERSTUFF * ALL CONTEST PARTICIPANTS GET FUN SURPRIZES!

Extra-special thanks and gifts also for two special earthkins:

1. For the name 'SYNTIZZA' (Syntilla pizza):
Kanishk Shah, 10, Jamnabai Narsee School, Mumbai
2. For suggesting the word 'Mystery' in the title:
Devyani Saini, 12, Indus International School, Bangalore

taranauts

THE MYSTERY OF THE SYNTILLA SILVERS

For Leo,
Write and tell me
how you liked the books!
taranauts@gmail.com
Best wishes,
Roopa Pai

CHASE THE STARS AT

www.taranauts.com

Roopa Pai suspects she has alien blood, for two reasons. One, she loved history in school. And two, although an adult, she mostly reads children's books.

Roopa has won a Children's Book Trust award for science writing. Among her published works are a four-book science series, *Sister Sister* (Pratham Books), and two girl-power books, *Kaliyuga Sita* and *Mechanic Mumtaz* (UNICEF).

When she is not dreaming up plots for her stories, she goes on long solo bicycle rides, and takes children on history and nature walks in Bangalore. You can find her at *www.roopapai.in*.

taranauts

BOOK FIVE

THE RIDDLE OF THE SYNTILLA SILVERS

Roopa Pai

Illustrated by Priya Kuriyan

hachette INDIA

First published in 2011 by Hachette India
(Registered name: Hachette Book Publishing India Pvt. Ltd)
An Hachette UK company
www.hachetteindia.com

1

ISBN 978-93-50093-15-3

Hachette Book Publishing India Pvt Ltd,
4th & 5th Floors, Corporate Centre;
Plot No. 94, Sector 44; Gurgaon 122003, India

Typeset in Perpetua 13.5/16
By Eleven Arts, New Delhi

Printed and bound in India
by Manipal Technologies Ltd, Manipal

For Kun Tal
Brewer of endless
cha-patti-&-fudina-laced conversations

Magmacup
MegaStage
Zum Skar
Glo
Dazl
Syntilla
Magmalift
Shaap Azur

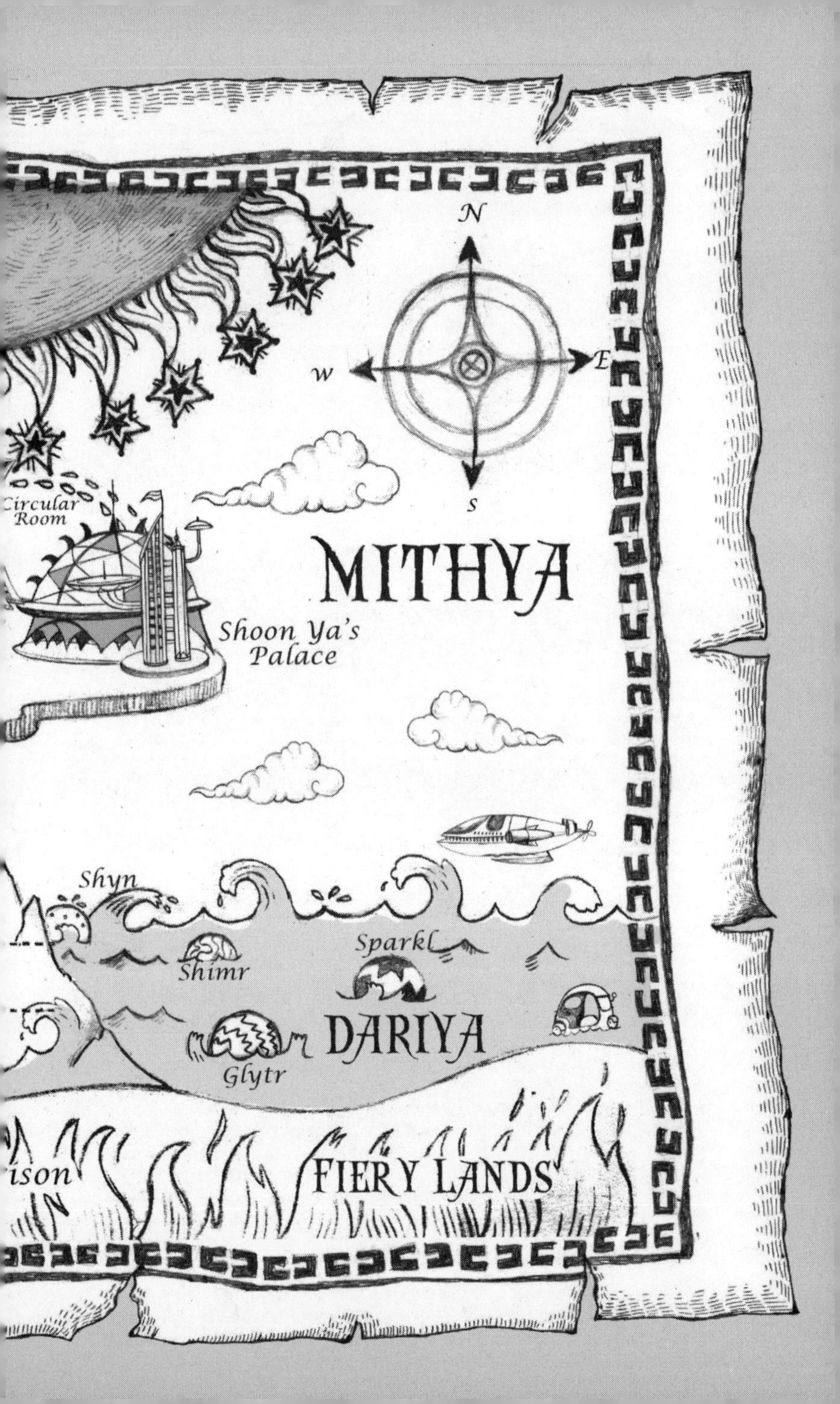
N
W
E
S
Circular Room
MITHYA
Shoon Ya's Palace
Shyn
Sparkl
Shimr
DARIYA
Glytr
ison
FIERY LANDS

The Trail of the Tale

Eight octons after the wise, brave Shoon Ya became Emperaza of Mithya, Mithya was celebrating with the grandest Octoversary ever. For the first time, the 32 stars of Tara—the supersun with the cool rainbow coloured light—had come down to dance at the celebrations. Until Shaap Azur, Shoon Ya's evil twin, broke out of his prison below the heaving seabed of Dariya and captured all 32 stars in the Silver Spinternet, plunging Mithya into darkness.

The stars could be rescued, but only if the 32 riddles Shaap Azur had hidden on the eight worlds were solved within an octet. Enter sweet-faced Zvala, child of Fire, athletic Zarpa, child of the superserpent Shay Sha, and animal magnet Tufan, child of the Wind—three gifted mithyakins who had been chosen by the Emperaza several octons ago to save Mithya from the Great Crisis.

Under the watchful eye of Shuk Tee, the Emperaza's most trusted advisor, and the guidance of expert

Achmentors—hypnotic Achalmun, who trains their minds, scatterbrained Dummaraz, who strengthens their values, full-of-fun Twon d'Ung, who fine-tunes their bodies, and brilliant Aaq, master of gizmotronics—the Taranauts begin to blossom into brave, strong, smart heroes.

For their first challenge, the Taranauts travelled to Shyn. After many exciting adventures, they cracked the hidden riddles and rescued the Emeralds. An octoll later, in Lustr's brain-scrambling Mayazaal, they battled flesh-eating flowers, weeping trees and hostile minimits in the company of their mysterious new friend Zubremunyun, before they set the Sapphires free.

In Sparkl, they had to play—and win—four deadly games to save the Amethysts. In the end, the Taranauts' winning mix of superskills, razor-sharp intelligence, and heart, combined with superb teamwork, saw them through. On to Glo, where, aided by a giant endangered hakibyrd, teen pop diva Dana Montana, and Tufan's beloved older brother, Dada, the Taranauts succeeded in outwitting a treacherous Marani to return the Rubies to their place in the sky.

One traitor has been unmasked, but Shuk Tee is convinced there are more. As the stakes get higher and anxiety grips both Zum Skar and XadYantra, the Taranauts set off for their next challenge—rescuing the Silvers. But will they be up to it?

Now read on . . .

Mithyology

Mithya A whole different universe, with eight worlds—Dazl, Glo, Shyn, Shimr, Lustr, Sparkl, Syntilla, Glytr—that bob around in the endless sea of **Dariya**, around the bad-tempered volcano **Kay Laas**. On top of Kay Laas, in the Land of Eternal Taralite, lives Shoon Ya, the Emperaza of Mithya.

Tara The rainbow-coloured supersun of Mithya. Tara is made up of 32 stars—the Emeralds, the Sapphires, the Amethysts, the Rubies, the Citrines, the Silvers, the Turquoises, and the Corals—in 8 iridescent colours.

Taraday A day on Mithya. It is 48 dings long.

Taralite From 1 o'ding to 32 o'ding, the **Upsides** of the eight worlds, where most mithyakos live, stay out of the water and enjoy the cool light of the Tarasuns, the stars of Tara. This part of the Taraday is called Taralite.

Fliptime At 32 o'ding, all the worlds flip over into Dariya. The moment when this happens is called Fliptime.

Taranite From Fliptime until 48 o'ding, the Upsides are turned away from Tara and into Dariya. During this time, they are in darkness, their buildings and vehicles and forests protected with water-repelling force-fields called Dar-proofs.

Downsides The halves of each world that stay in darkness, inside Dariya, for 32 dings each Taraday. These are scary, unexplored places, populated by creatures of the darkness and not-so-nice mithyakos.

Xad Yuntra The secret hideout of Shaap Azur, Emperaza Shoon Ya's evil twin.

Zum Skar The training centre at the Land of Eternal Taralite where the brightest mithyakos hone their skills. The Taranauts are now in training there.

Magmalift A magma-powered elevator inside Kay Laas in which mithyakos can zoom up to the Land of Eternal Taralite.

Aquauto An amphibious cab with the ability to travel both on water and on land. Aqualimos are the fancier version.

Stellipathy The technique of communicating directly through the mind.

Stellikinesis The technique of moving objects by force of will.

Stelliportation The technique of getting to another location without physically making the journey.

Hovitation The technique of staying in mid-air for several dinglings at a time.

One

'Zarpa, Zarpa!' Zvala shook her head mournfully at her friend. 'What am I going to do with you?'

Zarpa grinned and ran up to join Zvala at the Magmalift. She looked as tomboyish as ever, in her old pair of orange cargotrax with a hazillion pockets, a black dri-eazy stretch tee, and her black All-Terrain Obverse Nanos. 'You didn't seriously think I was going to change my wardrobe just because you and Dana thought I should, did you?'

'No-*oh,* but I was hoping you would have at least left the purple glolights in your hair—they looked so *cute* on you! And they last for over an octoll if you don't shampoo.'

'Not shampoo for a whole *octoll*?' said a horrified voice, as the third Taranaut arrived, swathed in a cloud of Max deo. 'I guess that's all right for people who don't mind smelling like a pandi-sty,' he threw Zvala a significant

glance, 'but Zarpa and I have different standards of personal hygiene, thanks.'

'And who, may I ask,' Zvala turned on Tufan, pinching her nose between her fingers, 'was talking to *you*, Mr Biggest-Stinkeroo-of-Them-All?'

'I will have you know,' lied Tufan smoothly, 'that your Suntana friend actually thought I had good taste in deo. She told me so herself.'

'As *if!*' retorted Zvala, although the tiniest doubt had crept into her mind—did Dana really think that? Maybe she, Zvala, was out of touch with what was 'in' on Mithya, then.

'Ask her if you like,' Tufan said airily. 'You, I'm afraid, are sadly behind the times.'

'Really?' Zvala's face fell.

'Shut up, Tufan,' Zarpa kicked Tufan in the shin. 'He's just teasing you, sillykoof—can't you tell?'

'Gahahahaa! Got you!' Tufan was convulsed with laughter.

'You horrible, lying, stinkyboochi! Wait till I . . .'

'Magmalift's here!' yelled Zarpa, quickly hustling her teammates into it. Zvala continued to yell, but mercifully, the roar of the Magmalift drowned out her words, making her look like a very grumpy meenmaach.

Here we go again, chuckled Zarpa to herself. She sighed happily—sure, the next few octolls would be filled with far more dangers than the Taranauts had faced before, but there was something reassuring about the things that didn't change—the Magmalift taking them back to Zum Skar, Zvala and Tufan squabbling, Achmentor Twon d'Ung and Makky waiting to receive them at the top . . .

As she stepped out of the Magmalift into the Land of Nevernite, she wondered what the mood would be like at Zum Skar now. The last octoll they had spent here, things had been weird, to say the least, with everyone nervous and talking in whispers and looking as if they had a big fat scary secret they couldn't share.

Beep. 1 New Call-Out.

Zarpa switched on her summoner, wondering idly where Twon d'Ung was and who the two uniformed mithyakos walking towards them were.

'Taranauts,' Shuk Tee's lilting voice floated out of the summoner, sounding grim. 'Two of Chief Sey Napati's men will receive you at the Magmalift and escort you to Zum Skar. Once you are here, go to your rooms, and stay there. Do *not* walk around unsupervised. Lunch will be served in your rooms. You will be picked up at 18 o'ding and brought to the Circular Tower Room. I will see you there.'

Huh? The Taranauts exchanged startled glances. Things at Zum Skar had definitely taken a turn for the worse.

The Taranauts huddled together nervously in the middle of the Tower Room, waiting. Cool emerald, sapphire, amethyst and ruby light spilled in from all four directions, bathing the room in a lovely, sparkly glow. Usually, the sight of the 16 rescued Tarasuns would have filled Zarpa with joy, but this time, they only reminded her that there were another 16 Tarasuns to go, *sixteen*!

She was so preoccupied that she noticed Shuk Tee only when she was already inside the room. The others looked startled too. 'Hello, Ms Shuk Tee,' they chorused, snapping to attention.

'Hello, Taranauts!' A rare smile broke across Shuk Tee's face. 'Cheer up! Surely I'm not *that* scary?'

The tension dissolved. The Taranauts relaxed. 'Well, Ms Shuk Tee,' said Zvala, her voice mildly accusing, 'it was you who started it by sending us that weird message . . .'

'What weird message?' Shuk Tee raised her eyebrows.

'You know, the one about how we should never go anywhere unsupervised and how we should wait for Chief Sey's men to escort us here, and . . .'

Shuk Tee's eyes gleamed. 'Oh, *that*,' she dismissed, smiling. 'One can never be too careful these days, you know . . . Now tell me, which world were you planning to tackle next?'

'Well,' began Zarpa, 'we haven't decided for certain yet, but we were thinking it might be . . .' Her mouth fell open. Shuk Tee had disappeared. The next moment, the door swung open and she walked in again, arms laden with dingplans.

'Hello, Taranauts,' she said briskly. 'Congratulations on a wonderful job.' She stopped, catching sight of their stunned faces, and frowned. 'What's the matter? You look like you've seen a ghost.'

'Uhhh . . . weren't you here just a moment ago, Ms Shuk Tee?'

'What do you mean? I just walked in, did I not?' She paused, suddenly alert. 'There was someone here *before* I walked in?'

'Yes, ma'am,' said Tufan. '*You* were.'

Shuk Tee drew a sharp breath. 'A Morphoroop!' she muttered, almost to herself. That meant the safety shield around Zum Skar had been breached! No ordinary Morphoroop could have done it, and even the best would have needed help from someone on the inside, but how . . . She saw the Taranauts looking at her with scared, wide-open eyes, and quickly composed herself.

'You are not to concern yourselves with this,' she said firmly. 'Leave this to me and Chief Sey. Your responsibility is to concentrate on perfecting your skills and on learning

everything your Achmentors can teach you. Here are your dingplans—this octoll will not be easy. It will need all the effort you can give.'

The Taranauts nodded slowly.

' As I was saying when I came in,' continued Shuk Tee, more gently, 'you mithyakins were fantastic in Glo. Great job with the Bay Runda, Tufan. Zarpa, impeccable leadership.' Tufan and Zarpa flushed happily.

'And you, Zvala,' Shuk Tee continued as Zvala looked up expectantly, 'have a real talent. Lt Muntri stellipathed me a freezeframe of the makeovers. These two almost looked, um, *respectable*, thanks to your efforts.'

'Really, Ms Shuk Tee?' Zvala cracked a huge grin and turned triumphantly to Zarpa and Tufan. '*Told* you!'

The edges of Shuk Tee's mouth twitched slightly. 'Run along now, Taranauts. Your first session is in a ding from now, and I believe there is a certain someone in the royal stables waiting impatiently to meet you.'

'Makky!' chorused the Taranauts, their faces lighting up at the thought of the big, affectionate makara. 'See you later, Ms Shuk Tee!'

'I have first dibs on Makky!' yelled Tufan, as they raced out of the Tower Room. 'He loves me the most!'

'Hah!' retorted Zarpa, zigzagging furiously away. 'Only if you can get there before me, loser!'

Two

'BWAHAHAHA!' guffawed Raaksh, wiping the tears from his eyes. 'Oh, it was priceless! You should have been there, sis! The brats' mouths fell open, like this,' he paused to demonstrate, 'when the real Madame Snootums walked in. I was still there in the room, only I had morphed into a little makdiboochi on the floor. It would have been a real shame to miss their expressions.'

Shurpa rolled her eyes discreetly as she listened to her brother tell the same story for the mazillionth time. Much as she hated to admit it, her brother was just a little—how could she put it—*dumb*. But he was also, like her, one of Mithya's best Morphoroops. Oh, there were others, of course, who had honed their skill through octons of dedication and practice, but she and Raaksh—they were *naturals*. That was what made them so valuable to the Master.

'And?' Paapi shrugged off her BattleWii gamesuit and hummonica, logged out of the simulagamer, and raised an enquiring eyebrow. 'Had Eye-in-the-Sky done his—or her—job on the safety shield?'

'Who? Oh, our spy in Kay Laas. Yes, he had. My tricks alone would have been no match for the shield.'

'A rather empty victory, then,' said a quiet voice from the other side of the room.

Raaksh turned towards it, furious. 'Hold your tongue, old man!' he raged. 'No one asked for your opinion.'

'Don't waste your breath, Raaksh,' spat Shurpa. 'The crotchety old fossil knows his days are numbered. He is only here on the Master's sufferance, and even I can tell that it is wearing a little thin now.'

The door swung open. It was Ograzur Dusht. 'What news do you bring, Raaksh? Which world are the Tarabrats travelling to next?'

'Oh, it was priceless, Dusht . . .' began Raaksh. Shurpa threw him a warning glance—Dusht would have no patience with elaborate explanations. Raaksh stopped. 'I mean, um, well, I didn't spend too much time . . .'

'Where. Are. They. Going. Next?' said Dusht slowly, biting off the words one by one.

'They . . . they hadn't decided yet.' The words came out in a rush.

'Well, you'd better stick with them until they do, then,' Dusht waggled an imperious forefinger. 'Because if there is one thing the Master cannot tolerate, it's incompetence.'

'Um, Dusht, you are such a good stellipath—can you not just use your skills to find out what they're thinking?' whined Raaksh. 'Do I really have to stelliport to where they are every time? It isn't easy, you know, with the safety shield and all . . .'

'What are you, Raaksh—*stupid*?' hissed Dusht. Shurpa bristled on her brother's behalf, but kept her silence. 'Do you know how much energy it takes me to untangle mithyakin thought skeins from all the other thought strands that choke the air of Mithya? The Master relies on me for too many things—I can't be wasting my time and energy doing someone else's job. *Especially* when that someone else,' he glared contemptuously at Raaksh, 'has no other talent the Master can use.'

His eyes roamed the room, and came to rest on Paapi. 'BattleWii? *Again*?' he sounded incredulous. 'The real battle is out there, my friend, not inside your simulagamer.' His voice rose. 'Get back to work! Everyone!' He turned and strode from the room.

Paapi scowled. 'Someone needs to tell Dusht where to get off,' she said. 'He is getting too big for his boots.'

'I agree,' said Shurpa, and Raaksh nodded. 'The Master will not listen to a word against him, though. I vote we speak to Hidim Bi—she will know what to do.'

In the corner of the room, Vak smiled to himself.

'The captive will not say a word, Emperaza,' Chief Sey Napati threw up his hands. 'I have tried everything that is within the bounds of the law—persuasion, threats, bribes, solitary confinement—but the Marani refuses to reveal who sent the summoners to Glo. We could try gentle torture next, and then gradually go on to . . . .'

'No!' said Shoon Ya firmly. 'We will never stoop to the kind of behaviour that we accuse the Downsiders of.' He turned to Shuk Tee. 'We will just have to find other ways to unmask the traitor in our midst.'

Shuk Tee nodded. 'And we have to keep the Taranauts safe, at all costs. We can't do much to protect them when they are away from here—the Marazas will do that—but if we can't keep them safe in Zum Skar, we will have really failed them.' She paused. 'There was a Morphoroop in the Tower Room this morning.'

Shoon Ya's eyebrows shot up. Chief Sey looked thunderstruck. 'This is too much!' he sputtered. 'The Downsiders are getting too bold. Sir, request permission to arrest prime suspect and throw him into prison.'

Shoon Ya's eyebrows scooted even higher. 'You already have a *prime* suspect, Chief? And who might that be?'

'Whoever programmed the summoners that were sent to Glo—and weakened the safety shield today—has to be an expert at gizmotronics,' shrugged Chief Sey. 'That makes Achmentor Aaq the prime suspect. It's pretty simple when you think about it.'

'There are a couple of things wrong with that theory,' Shuk Tee said slowly. 'First, Achmentor Aaq is not even in Zum Skar at the moment. He only returns here later this evening.' Chief Sey looked startled, then a little annoyed. 'I didn't know that.'

'Secondly,' continued Shuk Tee, 'You may recall that Zum Skar has its own set of summoners that can function through any blackout at all. They were designed some octons ago—and three of those are missing from the store.'

'Which means,' concluded Shoon Ya, 'that *anyone* who had access to the store could have sent the summoners, not necessarily someone proficient enough to program them.'

'Exactly,' said Shuk Tee. 'And as for the safety shield, I can think of several mithyakos here—the four Achmentors, the three of us, the Biggabhejas in the Central Research Institute—who know how to weaken it—*and all of them have access to the store too*! We have never kept anything locked up at Zum Skar.'

Chief Sey looked stumped for a moment. 'Be that as it may,' he continued stubbornly. 'I just have a hunch about Achmentor Aaq.'

'The law of the land, Chief,' said ShukTee sternly, 'does not brand anyone a criminal on the basis of someone's "hunch". Every mithyaka is innocent until proven guilty, and has a right to a fair trial.'

Chief Sey turned a dull, angry red under his skin, but he did not retort. He avoided ShukTee's eyes and turned to the Emperaza. 'As per orders, everyone in Zum Skar is being watched, Sir. All security has been tightened and the Black Bekkats are on standby. I shall await further orders. ' He bowed stiffly and withdrew.

ShukTee shut the door behind him. 'Before you accuse me of being rude to the Chief, Emperaza,' she said quickly, 'let me say this in my defence. I happen to know exactly where Chief Sey's "hunch" about Achmentor Aaq comes from.' ShoonYa waited.

'Before Sey joined the Mithsafety forces, he worked for the super-successful gizmotronic company, In4sys. He was a star there, expected to become their youngest CGO—Chief Gizmotronics Officer. Just before the company made the decision, another application for the post arrived. This second applicant came highly recommended from the Head Achmentor of the University of Kay Laas. The Achmentor argued that because his student came from difficult circumstances, he needed the job more. In the end, In4cys chose the second applicant.'

'Whose name, I presume, was Aaq Vis Ling?'

Shuk Tee nodded. Shoon Ya smiled wryly. 'Is there *anything* you don't know, Shuk Tee?'

'Not really. Which is why you should trust me.' Shuk Tee's face was impassive, but her eyes twinkled.

Shoon Ya knew what she was referring to—the fact that, three octolls ago, he had dismissed her conviction that there was a traitorous VIM on the loose. Until, of course, the Marani of Glo had been captured. 'Go on, then, Shuk Tee,' he sighed. 'Say it.'

'Say what? I told you so?' said Shuk Tee, tongue firmly in cheek. 'Emperaza, you know I would *never* stoop so low.'

Three

The Taranauts stood in the darkened room, staring hard at the three glowing balls on the floor at the other end. Achmentor Achalmun stood in a corner, watching them. 'Absolute focus,' he intoned. They tensed, waiting. 'Tufan—*hovitate*!'

'Come on, come on, come on,' muttered Tufan, as Achalmun set the balls rolling towards him. '*Now!*' The next dingling, Tufan rose into the air. One ball rolled away under his feet, two, th . . . *Bump*! Tufan came down hard on the third ball. Achalmun glared at him.

'Zarpa—go!'

The balls began to roll towards Zarpa, picking up speed. Zarpa focused with all her might. 'Now!' she cried, and rose into the air. The first ball rolled under her feet untouched, then the second, and the . . . Zarpa hit the floor one nanoding after the third had rolled past.

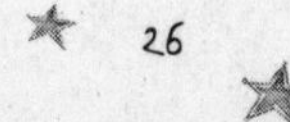

'Good effort!' growled Achalmun. 'Zvala—go!'

Zvala forced herself to concentrate. 'Now!' She rose into the air, pushing out all thoughts from her head. But one sidled in anyway. 'Whatever you do,' it said sneakily. 'You're never going to make this guy happy.' Her heart sank. The next instant, she lost focus, and dropped to the floor, right on top of the third ball.

Uh-oh. This would not do, this would not do at all. Zvala kept her eyes firmly averted from Achalmun's. She would have to come up with something a lot more impressive, and quickly, or she would never hear the end of it. What if she . . . yes, it *was* an idea . . . stellikinesis and hovitation combined!

Quickly, she focused on the glowing balls, willing them to roll towards her again. Like magic, the balls aligned, and began to roll. 'Now!' yelled Zvala, rising into the air. The first ball rolled untouched under her feet, and the second, and the third. One of them ricocheted off the opposite wall, and rolled back under a still-hovitating Zvala.

'Ufffff!' Zvala exhaled mightily as she hit the ground. Tufan and Zarpa burst into spontaneous applause. 'How did you *do* that?'

Zvala smiled nervously at her teammates, then stared at the floor and waited for Achalmun's response. Would he think she had been too cheeky? 'Doubt arises,' accused Achalmun, looking very displeased. 'Focus vaporizes.'

Zvala sighed. The Achmentor had read her mind, as usual. He was right to rebuke her too—after all those dings and dings of practice, she had let her concentration flag *again*. She looked up to apologize, and caught her breath. Achalmun's attention was elsewhere, but the swirling indigo-gold tattoo on his forehead had morphed into a pair of hands, and they were cheering her effort—with applause!

Achmentor Dummaraz bustled into the room, escorted like everyone else by two beefy mithyakas from the Mithsafety forces. 'Hello, mithyakins!' he greeted them, his glasses slipping off his nose, his pajamas flapping. 'What terrible times we live in, eh? Terrible times! Never in my long life have I had to be escorted everywhere by . . . by *brutes* like these . . . as if I were a common criminal. Never in my illustrious career of serving the Emperaza have I been suspected of being a traitor . . . A *traitor*! *Me*!'

The Taranauts exchanged glances in sudden understanding. So *that* was what it was all about, all the restrictions, all the rules about not going anywhere without an escort. It was as much to protect them as it was to keep tabs on everyone else. It also meant that there was *another* traitor around, and, horror of horrors, he or she was here, at Zum Skar!

Tufan turned to Dummaraz. 'I'm sure no one believes you are a traitor, Achmentor,' he said soothingly. 'The Emperaza and Chief Sey are only concerned about your safety. You are one of the most important mithyakos in Zum Skar, after all . . .'

Dummaraz stopped fussing with his things, as if arrested by the novel idea. 'Do you think so, mithyakin? Do you really think so? Yes, you may be right, at that . . . But if that were true, who *is* the traitor?'

This was just the opening Tufan was waiting for. 'What do you think, Achmentor? Our Emperaza is good, and wise, and fair—why would anyone wish him ill?'

Dummaraz considered the problem. 'Well, it isn't always that straightforward, you know,' he mused, 'It isn't always about wishing the Emperaza ill.' The Taranauts gathered around his table, listening. 'There could be so many other reasons for people to go over to the other side—greed, ambition, loyalty to another, belief in a cause, a feeling of being neglected by this side . . .' He paused. 'And, of course, the most powerful, most dangerous reason of all—love.'

'Love?' chorused the Taranauts.

'Yes, mithyakins, love,' sighed Dummaraz. 'But I don't expect you to understand, yet.'

'But there is no one on Zum Skar who is greedy or ambitious or who believes in Shaap Azur's cause, is there, Achmentor?' tried Tufan again.

'Ah, little ones, there are many dark secrets in every mithyaka heart,' said Dummaraz, pushing up his spectacles and arranging his palmyra scrolls busily.

Zarpa tried another tack. 'Why does the Emperaza think there is a spy here, Achmentor?'

'Well,' said Dummaraz, turning his head completely around in his unnerving way and beginning to write on the blackboard, 'there were those three summoners that were apparently sent from Kay Laas to Glo for you to use, but the Emperaza certainly hadn't asked for them to be sent. The Morphoroop that appeared in the Tower Room this morning—that could never have happened unless someone had weakened the safety shield from the inside. But you know all this, don't you?'

The Taranauts instantly wiped off their stunned expressions. 'Of *course*, Achmentor!'

'So what do *you* think?' Dummaraz looked at them, his usually vacant eyes suddenly crafty. 'Who is the traitor?'

'Well,' began Zvala, 'if you ask me . . .'

'Who can tell, Achmentor?' cut in Zarpa smoothly.

'What I would like to know,' continued Tufan, picking up the cue, 'is why that cunning lomdox—the Marani of Glo—turned traitor. She had *everything*!'

'Ah-ah, mithyakin,' chided Dummaraz, eyes glazing over again as he contemplated the issue, 'so quick to judge, are we not? On the one hand, yes, the Marani had everything—youth, beauty, power. On the other hand, she did not have enough—at least in her opinion—of the one thing she never had growing up—money. It was the only thing that would make her feel safe, and she wanted a lot of it. If you had had a kinhood like hers—stolen away from your family by a troupe of travelling gymnacrobats, forced to perform each nite for a few stale creposas, never having a thing to call your own until you were old enough to escape—maybe you would not be so harsh. Maybe you would even feel a tinge of admiration for what she managed to achieve for herself before . . . before *this*.'

'There aren't always two sides to everything, Achmentor Dummaraz,' said Tufan fiercely. 'Some things are just *wrong*.'

A look of real fear jumped into Dummaraz's eyes. It was gone in a flash, but all the Taranauts had seen it. They wondered what or who the Achmentor was afraid of.

Four

'Excellent!' said Achmentor Aaq, nodding approvingly at the mini jet-pack Tufan had assembled out of the bits and bobs the Achmentor had handed out to all of them at the beginning of the session. Zarpa and Zvala were still hard at work at their tables, struggling to make sense of Aaq's 'simple' circuitograms.

'Uffpah!' sighed Zvala. 'This is just no good. I have no idea where this little thingummy goes or what this zigzaggy line is supposed to stand for . . .'

'Neither do I,' groaned Zarpa. 'It's completely useless.'

'It's sad but true,' shrugged Achmentor Aaq, smiling his annoyingly superior smile, 'girls just don't seem to have a flair for gizmotronics.' From behind his back, Tufan imitated Aaq's shrug and threw up his hands in mock-resignation. Zarpa and Zvala glared at him.

'Tell you what,' continued Aaq. 'Leave your kits be for a dingling and come and watch Tufan launch his jet-pack. Maybe you will be inspired.'

The girls didn't need to be told twice—anything to get away from those irritating itty-bitty integrated chiplets and shiny cuprowires.

In the garden, Tufan strapped the jet-pack to a shardula action figure he was carrying in his pocket, placed it on the ground at the perfect angle for take-off, and stepped back, flight controller in hand. 'ten, nine, eight . . .'

The jet-pack began to hum like a mudhoomakbee, its pitch steadily rising. 'three, two, one . . . aaaaand blast-off!' Lytazer beams shot out of the twin engines of the jet-pack, singeing the blue grass, as the shardula zoomed skywards. 'Hurrrayyy!' yelled Tufan, dancing a little jig. Two dinglings later, its little fuel-tanks depleted, the jet-pack fell back to the grass. The shardula shattered.

'I see great potential here,' said Aaq, clapping Tufan on the back. 'Whenever you have the time, I'd be happy to give you some extra lessons. And you are welcome to come and mess around in my lab anytime.' Tufan's eyes bulged out of his head. 'That would be just . . . just . . . mastastic, Achmentor,'

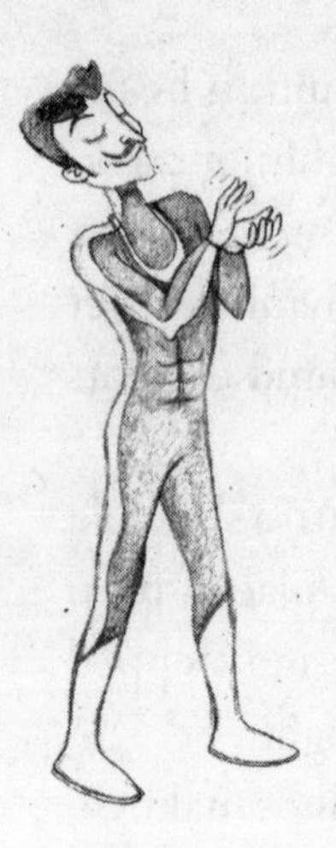

he stuttered. 'Thanks so very much. And, Achmentor,' he continued hurriedly, before Aaq got lost in himself and his genius again, 'how's MISTRI going?'

'Oh, that's going superbly, as you can expect when I'm in charge,' boasted Aaq, delighted to be talking about his latest greatest invention—the Molecular-level Imaging for Seamless Translocation and Reconstruction Interface, MISTRI for short. Using MISTRI, three-dimensional objects could be converted into two-dimensional pictures, and *back again*, making large objects incredibly easy to transport and retrieve. 'In fact, I had a bit of a lucky break a few octites ago and cracked one of the biggest glitches in the product, so it is almost ready to launch. A few more trials, of course, but that's a mere formality, just so that the dunderhead Biggabhejas at the Mithya Research Institute are satisfied.'

'And . . . and . . . you think I could help out with some of those trials?'

'I don't see why not,' Aaq shrugged. 'Every genius needs his worker mudhoomakbees.' He whirled to face the girls, releasing a great whiff of sharp, too-sweet deo. They crinkled their noses automatically. 'You girls! Back to your kits. And I want to see results this time!' He walked back into the classroom, checking his reflection in his summoner as he went.

'Ms Twon d'Ung!' Zvala's voice was triumphant as she galloped towards her teacher, having successfully taken her ashvequin through the tough obstacle course for the very first time. Zarpa and Tufan could do the course in their sleep now, of course, but for Zvala, this was huge. '*Ms Twon d'Ung*!'

Twon d'Ung looked up, startled. 'You weren't watching me at all, were you?' accused Zvala, dismounting expertly. 'You were lost again in the Land of Far Far Away!'

Twon d'Ung looked very guilty. 'I guess I was,' she said apologetically. 'I'm sorry, I really am. Will you do the course one last time? Please? I won't take my eyes off you for an instant. I promise.'

Zvala was still peeved, but she mounted her ashvequin again and rode off. What was wrong with their favourite Achmentor? She had such a worried, pinched look about her these days, and she didn't seem interested in anything they had to say anymore.

However, when she came galloping back, having completed the course perfectly for the second time, Twon d'Ung was beaming. Zarpa and Tufan were there too, having just ridden there on the Makkybus.

'Well, well, well,' Twon d'Ung smiled, shaking her head. 'We have come a long way, haven't we? From being terrified of ashvequins and hating anything that even smelled like exercise to—this! Well done, Zvala!'

'Yeah, yeah,' dismissed Tufan, pulling Makky's ears affectionately. 'She still sucks at gizmotronics, though. They both do, actually. Not their fault, of course—' his

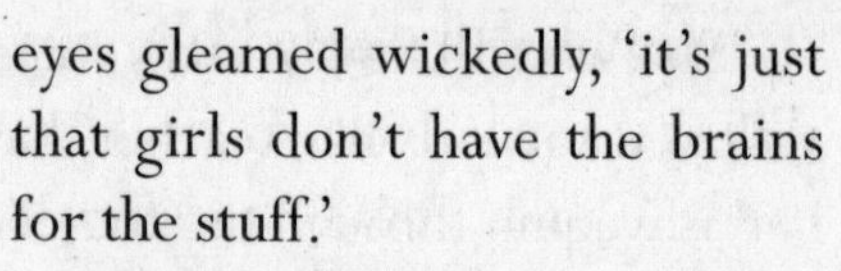

eyes gleamed wickedly, 'it's just that girls don't have the brains for the stuff.'

'That's rubbish!' Twon d'Ung turned on Tufan fiercely. 'I never thought I'd hear *you* say that, Tufan, after all you've been through with these two. Where *do* you get these weird ideas from?'

'You tell him, Ms Twon d'Ung!' agreed Zvala, furious. 'Ever since our Mr Stinky became best friends with Achmentor Stinky, he thinks he is too good for the likes of us.'

'I agree,' scowled Zarpa. 'All Tufan does these days is repeat what Achmentor Aaq says—and it's all infuriating stuff like this. Our friend has no thoughts of his own anymore.'

'Whoaaaa!' said Tufan, a little surprised at the amount of emotion his words had provoked. 'Surely you don't think I really meant what I said! Can't a guy *joke* around here anymore? *Sheeesh*!'

But Twon d'Ung was not mollified. 'I'm going to have a word with your Achmentor Aaq,' she said, her eyes sparking fire. 'He simply will not undermine my favourite girlkins this way.'

'Yayyyyy!' cheered Zvala and Zarpa.

'And he will surely listen to you, won't he, Ms Twon d'Ung?' sang Zvala, remembering what Twon d'Ung had told them about Aaq some octolls ago—that he had been her junior in school, and that it was she who had kept him in line then. 'Otherwise, just kick him in the shin at dinner!'

Twon d'Ung's eyes glazed over. 'I wonder,' she whispered, almost to herself. 'I wonder if he will still listen to me.' And then she was gone again, back to the Land of Far Far Away.

'This meeting will now come to order,' said Zarpa firmly, tapping her scratchscribe sharply against the headboard of her bed. Reluctantly, Tufan gave up trying to persuade Squik the Amazing Gileli to jump through the 'Ring of Fire', part of a miniature circus he had rigged up. Zvala, who had been drawing dots-and-stars patterns around her eyes with a stick of kankohl, sank on to the bed beside Zarpa, yawning. It was one ding to fliptime, and it had been another long, exhausting octite.

'There is only one item on the agenda today,' said Zarpa solemnly. 'We have to figure out which Tarasuns we will rescue next.'

'Before we begin,' said Zvala. 'Let's take precautions. First of all, we will lock the door.' She leaped off the bed, matching the action to the words. 'Second, we will repeat the Chant of Deep Stillness three times, and "erect fences, enclose thoughts", like Achmentor Achalmun taught us in Stellipathy yesterday. Three, we stellipath each other instead of talking—we definitely need the practice.'

Tufan groaned. 'Yes to one and two, but can we please, please not stellipath and just talk like normal mithyakins instead? I'm really bad at that stuff and you know it!'

'More reason for you to practice, then,' ruled Captain Zarpa mercilessly. 'Come on now, guys. Aaaaaaa . . . Uuuuuuu . . . Mmmmmm.'

Zvala focused hard, feeling the fences come up in her mind, enclosing her thoughts. Her fence, like the others', was still very fragile, no defence at all against a master stellipath, but she would get better with practice. *Ping! Ping!* Zarpa and Tufan had sent her mindchat requests. Zvala accepted instantly. Now, if none of them lost focus, their minds would only be accessible to each other.

'*So*,' said Zarpa, straight into her head, '*to which world are the Taranauts headed next?*'

'*I don't really care*,' she stellipathed back. '*I don't think there is really much to choose between them.*'

'*And no world is any darker than the others*,' added Zarpa.

'*Inki Pinki*,' said Tufan succinctly, unwilling to exert himself.

'*I suppose that's as good a method as any*,' grinned Zarpa. '*Here goes—starting with Dazl and going dingdial-wise. "Inki Pinki Pon-ki, Pappy had a monkapi, Monkapi died, Pappy cried, Inki Pinki Pon-ki"—Syntilla!*'

They all burst out laughing. 'That was easy!'

'*Syntilla tag?*' asked Tufan. '*Pain and peril*,' said Zvala instantly. Zarpa pinched her lip worriedly. '*What?*' said Zvala. '*Would you have rather chosen Manic Monsters, or Terror Trail, or Deadly Danger?*' Zarpa shrugged. '*I guess not.*'

'So quit thinking about it, then, worryboochi,' Tufan punched her on the shoulder, beginning to speak aloud again. 'And let's discuss something far more exciting—who is the traitor in Zum Skar?'

'My vote goes to Achalmun the Mean or Aaq the Vain,' Zvala thumped the bed. 'All in favour, say aye!'

'Nayyyyy!' yelled Tufan. 'Aaq has given us cool stuff to carry to our next mission, and as for Achalmun—don't you *dare* say a word against him! I think it might be . . .' he winked at Zvala, '. . . Twon d'Ung the Dreamy.'

'Nevvvahhhh!' Zarpa locked her feet around the headboard and stretch-leapt on Tufan, encircled him in her coils like a boaslith, and squeezed until he begged for mercy. Zvala hooted.

'Okay, okayyyy,' groaned Tufan, 'Not Twon d'Ung. Who's left? Dummaraz!'

There was a silence. Then Tufan the Fair jumped to the Achmentor's defence. 'Just because he is no one's favourite Achmentor does not make him a traitor, you know.'

'You're right,' sighed Zarpa. 'But it is all just too creepy. Except Ms Shuk Tee and the Emperaza, no one is *really* above suspicion. I just hope it turns out to be one of those Biggabhejas at the Research Institute or one of the guys from the Mithsafety forces, someone we don't know.'

'Maybe the traitor is not here at all and everyone is completely mistaken,' said Zvala slowly. 'Maybe the real culprit is—Zub the Mysterious!' The next instant, she found herself on her back, laughing and screaming, while two hard pillos whacked her from either side.

Five

'Syntilla,' said Zvala, reading from her wikipad, 'is lit by the Silvers, four Tarasuns that cast a cooler light than any of the others in the supersun Tara. As a result of the lower temperatures, the landscape is marked by snow-covered mountains, cold deserts, and frozen lakes. Syntilla used to be the snowsports capital of Mithya, and tourists from all over used to flock there in droves. But all that has changed since the Great Depressiccate.' Zarpa and Tufan looked at her quizzically.

'Until two octons ago,' Zvala continued reading, 'the Bisibrooks (Syntillian hot springs) waterway system was the life-blood of Syntilla. The canals of the waterway connected the four main urban centres—Ik, Do, Tin and Cha—allowing people and goods to travel easily between them. Forests and fields thrived along the fertile banks of the Bisibrooks, and the waters provided

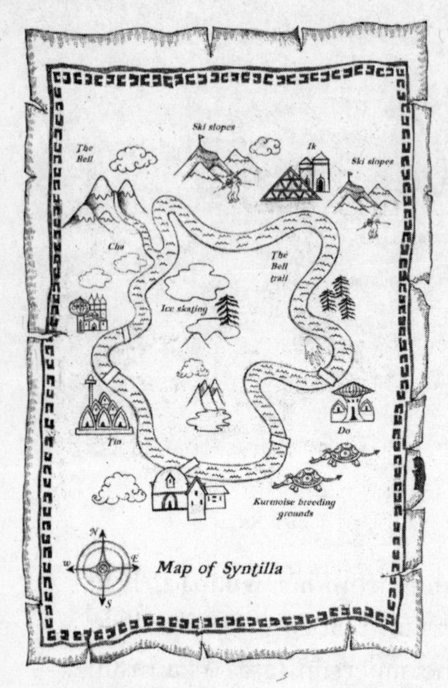

the perfect environment for the silverbacked kurmoises to spawn. Ever since the springs died out inexplicably, however—an event referred to as the Great Depressiccate—Syntilla has turned into a cold, barren wasteland, with Syntillakos mostly confined to their own towns.'

'And now the Silvers are gone too,' said Zarpa, staring out at Dariya from the window of their unmarked aqualimo. 'Poor things—maybe it was a good thing we chose to come here before the other worlds, after all.'

'What's a silverbacked kurmoise, anyway?' Zvala looked puzzled. 'And how do *they* affect anything?'

'A freshwater amphibian,' explained Tufan, 'with superb tracking abilities. On the highly endangered list ever since their breeding grounds—the Bisibrooks—dried up. They are adapted to a cold environment, so they can even follow a scent that's buried under several inches of snow. I remember Azza telling me about them—how, when he had visited Syntilla as a young man, he had travelled around in an aquasled pulled by kurmoises. Apparently, with all the snowfall here, that was the only way to make sure you didn't get lost when you were heading for the ski slopes or the frozen lakes. No kurmoises, no tourists.'

Zvala continued reading. 'The Syntillakos are an unusually tall race. Following the Great Depressiccate, most Syntillakos speak very little. Many suffer from severe depression. They can appear hostile or unfriendly to visitors.'

'Wow,' said Tufan. 'I like them already!'

There was a discreet knock on the door. 'Syntilla at starboard, Taranauts. Landfall in ten dinglings.'

The Taranauts rushed to the right side of the cabin, Tufan moving a little slower than the others. They peered out of the windows at the large landmass looming out of the water, feeling the familiar thrill of anticipation and anxiety. Zarpa peered at the beach—it was deserted. She heaved a sigh of relief. After the Bulletbiker episode at Glo, elaborate dockside receptions for the Taranauts had been completely banned, and what a good thing that was!

There was a gentle juddering as the aqualimo eased up the beach, folded in its sea-paddles, and popped its wheels out. Then they were on their way again, zipping through the dark, quiet streets towards the Maraza's palace. Tufan hobbled to the washroom—time to rain!

'Set up for stellipathy, team,' ordered Zarpa, as soon as Tufan returned. They had just finished testing the mindchat channels when the aqualimo rolled to a halt opposite a sparkling crystal structure that looked as if it grew right out of the ground. 'The Syntilla Palace,' announced the voice outside the door. The Taranauts stepped out, and gasped as a freezing blast of air hit them full in the face.

'That's c-c-c-old,' Zvala shivered mightily as the wind sliced right through her lacy white dress with the silver sequins, all the way to her bones. Zarpa and Tufan didn't bother to answer—their teeth were chattering too much.

A door opened in the structure, and a giant unsmiling mithyaka, clad from head to toe in a grey snugsuit, came striding out, his grey knee-length boots making no sound at all. A heavy sack swung easily from one of his fingers. Behind him came two others, one male, the other female, equally sombre, carrying a strangely-shaped tub. The giant stopped in front of the Taranauts and shook out the black sack. Out tumbled three small snugsuits exactly like his.

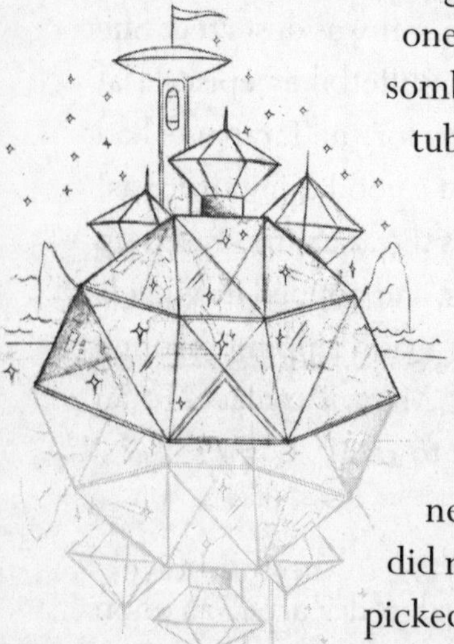

'Put them on,' ordered the mithyaka carrying the tub.

Wordlessly, and a little nervously—these guys definitely did not look friendly!—the Taranauts picked up the suits, and staggered back. *Whoaaa!* These were heavy! Would they even be able to move once they had them on? Amazingly, once they were worn, the suits moulded themselves to their bodies, and felt no heavier than dri-eazy tees! Instantly, the Taranauts were warm again. The other two giants approached now, and laid the steaming tub at their feet. A viscous black liquid swirled slowly in the tub, bubbling gently, reminding Tufan uncomfortably of Budbudana.

'Legs in,' said the mithyaki. Her voice was cheery and musical, completely at odds with her expression.

'What?! No way!' protested Tufan. 'I demand to see the Maraza before I put my feet into anything that looks like that.'

'The Maraza,' said the mithyaki, pointing to the mithyaka holding the sack.

The Taranauts stared. *Ping! Maraza, other Syntillakos, dress same-same?* Tufan sounded incredulous. *And Maraza carry heavy stuff? Himself-himself?* returned Zvala. Then she clenched her teeth. *Toooofaaan! Stop stellipathing like that! You're making me forget all my Taratongue grammar!* 'Your Starness,' Zarpa bowed, frowning at the others. The others followed, reddening.

'I'll go first,' said Zarpa, walking to the tub bravely and plunging her legs in right up to the knees. When she pulled them out again, they were coated in the black

stuff, which was solidifying rapidly. 'Warm boots,' said the mithyaki.

Zarpa walked around, trying them out. 'They're brilliant, Your Starness!' she exulted. 'I've never had such comfortable boots before!' *And I've never looked so much like a kakrow before!* groaned Zvala, as she pulled her legs out. *Black is so not my colour*. Tufan went next. *Love!* he stellipathed, striking a pose. *Black Avenger rides again!*

'Welcome,' said the mithyaka who wasn't the Maraza, 'to the Ice Palace.' The Taranauts goggled. That crystal structure—that was built of . . . ice? 'Your Starness . . .' began Zvala, but the conversation was over. The Maraza was already striding away towards the door. The Taranauts followed hurriedly, running a little to keep up, wondering what other surprises this strange world held for them.

Six

'Syntilla, eh?' said Shaap Azur, a slow smile spreading across his face. 'A world full of unhappy, brooding mithyakos. And for the last two octons, since the Great Depresiccate, a world full of angry and scared mithyakos—angry that the Emperaza isn't doing enough for them, scared that we are slowly but surely taking control. The brats will have their hands full this time.'

'They are not using summoners, Master,' continued Raaksh, looking concerned. 'The Emperaza has completely forbidden it, after what happened in Glo. So—how are we going to stay one step ahead of the brats this time?'

'Don't worry your poor little head about it, Raaksh,' cut in Dusht condescendingly. 'Do you think the Master had not anticipated this?' Raaksh flushed. Shurpa flashed Hidim Bi a look. Hidim Bi nodded, imperceptibly.

'You haven't answered the question, Dusht,' said Paapi sharply.

'There is no need for everyone in XadYuntra to know everything,' growled Dusht. 'All you need to know is that we've taken care of it.'

'We?' Hidim Bi raised her eyebrows. 'You see, Master, how the lowly kukcur, who used to be grateful for scraps from your table, now presumes to put himself on the same level as you! Learn to talk to the Master with respect, pup!'

Dusht shot out of his chair, the knuckles gripping the table white with rage. 'Shut your . . .'

'Quiet, Dusht!' roared Shaap Azur. 'Quiet, *all* of you!' His mouth curled contemptuously. 'This is what a general likes to see in the thick of battle, doesn't he, you sorry bunch? Division within the ranks!' He looked around the table, eyes boring holes in each of his Ograzurs. 'Here's my decision,' he brought his fist down on the table, making everyone jump. 'As of this dingling, Dusht takes over as my second-in-command—*and you will all report to him*.'

'May we know why the insolent pup was chosen, Master, when there are others more deserving?' ventured Hidim Bi boldly.

'Be-*cause*, my dear,' Shaap Azur bent down until his face was level with hers, 'because I say so.'

He paused to let his words sink in. 'If anyone around this table has any objections at all to this new appointment, he or she is free to leave Xad Yuntra now, and forever. Anyone?'

In the pin-drop silence that followed, a wizened hand went up. The Ograzurs gasped. For a fleeting moment, disbelief, pain, and something very like panic chased each other across Shaap Azur's handsome face. Then it was gone, replaced by the familiar anger and hardness. 'Go, then, Achmentor Vak!' he said, turning his back on his old teacher.

Ograzur Vak, his face suffused with sorrow, bowed and left the room. He would have liked to enclose his favourite student in a farewell hug, give him some parting words of advice, but this was not the time or place.

'Master, you are making a mistake!' Dusht sprang to his feet. 'Don't let the deserter go free! Throw him into the dungeons instead! You know what he will do the moment he walks out of the gates—join the Emperaza's forces, share our secrets . . .'

'Shut your mouth, Dusht. Achmentor Vak would never do that. And,' Shaap Azur's voice took on a menacing note, 'if I ever hear that any of you or

your cronies have bothered him in any way at all, the consequences are not going to be pretty. Now get out, all of you, back to your jobs—the brats must have already arrived.'

'Your rooms,' sang the giant mithyaki. The Taranauts stared at the two interconnected rooms, lit by a bluish glow. Strange shimmering rugs lay strewn on the floor and hung from the walls. They had complicated patterns woven into them with shiny red cuprowires that hummed and glowed with ionergy.

Ice beds—seriously??! groaned Zvala. 'Yes, seriously!' trilled the mithyaki cheerfully. 'But don't worry, Zvala, you will be very comfortable once you're tucked into your ionergized blankets.'

The giant mithyaka frowned at his companion. 'Less talk, Cha Patti,' he said shortly.

'Oh, *pshaw*, let me be, Tin Patti,' said the mithyaki fiercely. 'I am bored to tears here with you and the silent Maraza. Yeah, yeah, I know good Syntillakos are supposed to be all sad and silent, angry and depressed at our "fate", but I am not one of those, all right? Plus, there is finally, finally someone here who is happy and hopeful and . . . and will actually talk back to me! If you think I'm going to do the "less talk" thing while they are around, well, you've got another think coming!' She stopped suddenly, as if surprised by the length of her own speech. The mithyaka left the room, shaking his head in disgust.

The Taranauts stared, still taking in the fact that the giant mithyaki had so casually tuned into their stellipathic conversation. 'Oh, don't look at me like that!' sang the mithyaki. 'I don't bite! I know what you're thinking—I mean, *literally*, even when you're not stellipathing each other. I can't help it—I'm a Readakin.' They looked at her, eyes wide and uncomprehending.

'It's nothing scary, I assure you,' she went on hurriedly. 'It's just this gift I have, to be able to read mithyakin thoughtwaves.' She rolled her eyes. '*Some* gift! Mithyakins never stop thinking, so my head is always full of all this noise. But listen, you're not to tell anyone about it, okay? There are very, very few of us left

in Mithya and we keep our powers secret, because . . .' She cut herself short.

'Oh, we haven't even been properly introduced, have we? I know you guys, of course—I've heard so much about you, and I've been waiting and waiting for you all to come to Syntilla, and I'm going to take really good care of you . . .' She stopped herself again, with an effort, and held out a very large hand. 'Cha Patti.'

Zvala and Zarpa shook her hand, giggling. They liked this chatterbox mithyaki with the sing-song voice. Tufan smiled too. 'So the other guy,' he imitated his dour expression, 'your brother? Husband?'

'Him!' Cha Patti looked appalled. 'The very idea! We're not even remotely related!'

'But you have the same surname, don't you?'

Cha Patti looked puzzled for a dingling. 'Oh, no, no, no—it doesn't work that way on Syntilla,' she explained. 'Here the "surname" actually comes first. And there are only four popular surnames—Ik, Do, Tin and Cha.'

'Those are the big cities of Syntilla, right?' Cha Patti nodded. 'I am from Cha and he is from Tin, so those are our surnames. Unfortunately—' she sighed dramatically, 'both our first names are Patti.' The Taranauts digested this. 'And what if there is another Patti in Cha? Won't he or she also be called Cha Patti?' asked Zvala. 'Yes, it's all very confusing, since we don't have that many first names to choose from either. So there is usually a nickname. For instance, mine is . . .' she stopped, flushing.

Tufan grinned. 'Go on, tell us. Or wait, let me guess. Your full name is Cha "Blahdeblah" Patti.'

Cha Patti's mouth fell open. 'How did you *know*?' she breathed, looking at Tufan with a mixture of awe and fear.

'Oh, just a lucky guess!' shrugged Tufan, his eyes twinkling.

Cha Patti swallowed. 'They told me you mithyakins were smart, but I didn't know you were so . . . *scary* smart.'

Zarpa stifled a yawn. 'Oh, oh, where are my manners?' wailed Cha Patti. 'You poor little tykes must be so tired.' She rushed out of the room, and was back in a blink, carrying thick cuddlewool sheets and blankets, a Syntilla-sized pitcher of something that smelled absolutely delicious, and a large storipad. Quickly, she tucked each of them in and handed steaming mugs of fudgebutter flipfloat around. Zarpa sighed contentedly, feeling like she was back home in Lustr. *I could get used to this*.

Cha Patti opened the storipad. 'A bedtime tale,' she said. Her voice fell a couple of octaves. 'This is the story of a wicked wizard, a villain of the deepest dye . . .'

BOOOOOOM!

The storipad exploded in Cha Patti's hands. Hot fudgebutter flipfloat flew as the mugs shattered. 'Owww!' yelled Zarpa and Tufan as the scalding liquid splashed on their unprotected faces and fingers. Screaming with terror, Cha Patti ducked behind the ice beds. Unaffected by the heat of the explosion, Zvala leaped out of bed and into a defensive Kalarikwon position, fiery fingers at the ready for whatever was coming next.

Bzzzzt! One of the shimmering rugs on the wall had caught fire. The Taranauts coughed and sputtered as dense clouds of black smoke, reeking of burning cuddlewool, filled the room, making their eyes water. The rug crackled and fizzed, its edges curling and flaking as it fell to the icy floor. Immediately, the fire hissed and went out. The room was silent again.

Tufan and Zarpa were instantly at Zvala's side. Slowly, the smoke cleared. Still rigid from shock, Cha Patti peered over the top of the bed. Even though they were badly shaken themselves, the Taranauts had to suppress the urge to giggle at the sight of her large, powerful frame slowly emerging from its completely inadequate hiding place.

Zarpa was the first to recover. 'Taranauts,' she said, her voice grim. 'Knowing our friend Shaap Azur's methods, I'm betting our first challenge on Syntilla has just been delivered. But what is it?' Tufan raced to the fragment of

burnt rug and picked it up gingerly. The three of them bent over it, noticing how the cuprowires that had been woven into the pattern had warped and bent, creating an entirely new pattern.

'Hey, this looks like a circuitogram—a very cool one,' began Tufan, when he was interrupted by a shout from Cha Patti. The Taranauts whirled. With a shaking finger, she was pointing to the wall where the rug had been. The burning rug had melted the ice behind it unevenly, and a tightly rolled scroll of palmyra was now faintly visible, embedded in the icy wall. 'I'll get it!' yelled Zvala, shooting a concentrated heat beam directly at the wall. As the ice melted, she reached in, grabbed the scroll, and unrolled it.

'What's *that* supposed to mean?' said Tufan, sticking the bit of burnt rug into his pocket. When he got back to Kay Laas, he'd show it to Achmentor Aaq.

'It looks like complete gibberish,' agreed Zarpa

'Not now, not now, mithyakins,' Cha Patti bustled around, clearing bits of debris and chasing them into another set of rooms down the corridor. 'Straight to bed now—plenty of time tomorrow to figure the puzzle out. I'll bring you some fresh flipfloat, and I shall stay guard for the rest of the nite. Let anyone who dares disturb your sleep, beware the wrath of Cha Patti!'

She looked so fierce and determined that the Taranauts didn't have the heart to laugh. 'You go for it, Cha Patti!' said Tufan, as they filed out of the room. 'Oh, and can you please, please make my fudgebutter flipfloat a double?'

'I dreamt only in jumbled words all nite,' groaned Zvala, looking at the scroll the next morning. 'But this still makes no sense—*gah*!' They were sitting at a breakfast table hewn entirely out of ice, feasting on crisp, cheesy

slices of warm-from-the-oven Syntizza. The Maraza sat at the head of the table, watching them, with Tin Patti and Cha Patti, uncharacteristically silent, on either side.

'Maybe it is a code,' suggested Zarpa, 'where each letter actually stands for some other letter of the alphabet. Now, "e" is the most common letter in Taratongue, so whichever letter is repeated most often in the scroll would logically stand for "e".'

'Tried that already,' sighed Zvala. 'Guess which letter is repeated most often? E!'

'Oh.' Zvala looked sheepish. 'But doesn't it mean, then,' said Tufan, feeding Squik and Chik-Chik handfuls of the silvery barafberries that grew in such profusion both inside and outside the palace, 'that the message is in Taratongue itself?'

'Yes, that's what I was thinking,' frowned Zvala. 'Except it *isn't*! But sometimes, a perfectly normal sentence can seem like gobbledegook if the words are split differently. Like,' she pulled out a scratchscribe and a papyrus pad, scribbled a line, and held it out to the others—*whost hete amwi theb igbi gdre am*. 'Read that!'

'Words that are split differently,' said Zvala slowly. 'Oh, I get it! It reads—*Who's the team with the big, big dream!*'

'Hurray!' said Tufan. 'Except—*this* message doesn't make sense even when you split the words differently.'

He looked at the scroll again. 'I wonder what the deal is with the capital letters in the middle.'

'Me too,' agreed Zvala. 'The capital letters could indicate the beginning of a new line or sentence . . . but then why is the *last* letter a capital letter?'

'Maybe the capital letters indicate the end of a sentence, then?' suggested Tufan.

'Or maybe,' said Zarpa, 'you have to read the message *backwards*, from right to left . . .' The three of them stared at the scroll some more.

'Eeeeeeeee! That's it! That's it!' Zvala began to write furiously on her pad. 'Here it is—the whole message!'

From Ik to Cha, there leads a trail
A trail that's fraught with much travail
Traverse it! The Silvers shall be revealed
When the cracked silver bell has pealed

'Oh Chik, oh Squik, to Ik, to Ik!' chortled Tufan. *Ping! Behave, sillykoof! The Maraza's here*! Tufan, who had completely forgotten the Maraza's presence, had the grace to look embarrassed.

The Maraza signalled to Tin Patti. He nodded. 'Snowbamba waiting,' he said. 'Driver knows the route to Ik. The Bell Trail leads out of the city's eastern end.'

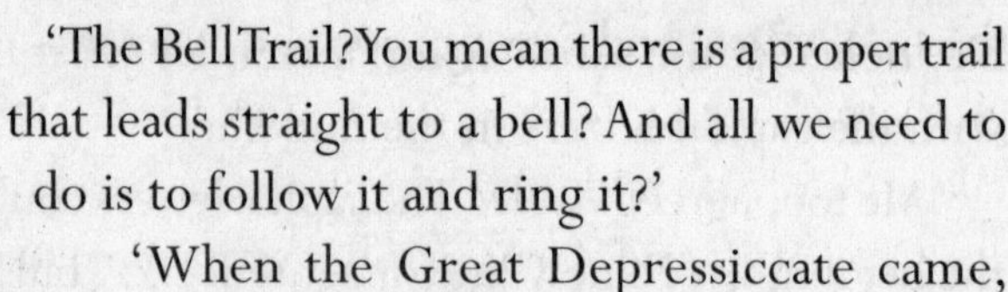

'The Bell Trail? You mean there is a proper trail that leads straight to a bell? And all we need to do is to follow it and ring it?'

'When the Great Depressiccate came, the bell went silent,' explained Tin Patti. 'The trail has not been used since. The trail markers may have disappeared.'

Cha Patti cleared her throat. 'Dangers on the trail,' she said cryptically. Tin Patti frowned at her. 'Less talk, Cha Patti.'

'What kinds of dangers?' demanded Tufan. 'We need to know if we are to be prepared.'

But Tin Patti would not explain. The Maraza stood up, shook hands solemnly with all of them and left, followed by Tin Patti. Cha Patti waited until they had left the room, then burst into musical speech.

'Yes, there is a trail. Yes, the bell at the end doesn't ring anymore. Many people think the bell is haunted and that the evil spirit in the bell caused the Depressiccate, so no one goes there anymore. A few octons ago, a team of Biggabhejas set out along the trail to prove that all the "haunted bell" stories were rubbish. They believed the trail had in fact been booby-trapped by Downsiders who wanted to scare us into going over to their side. But the Biggabhejas never came back. After that, of course . . .'

She wrung her hands. 'If we only had three pairs of kurmoises, they would have pulled your sled straight to the bell without missing a step, but no one knows where to find them anymore. And now my poor little mithyakins have to go there alone . . . Tell you what—I'll come with you and take care of you and tuck you into your beds . . .'

'Cha Patti!' said Zarpa firmly, cutting her off mid-flow. 'You have to stop worrying about us. We are the Taranauts, remember? We can take care of ourselves.'

Cha Patti's face fell. 'I guess so,' she said glumly, 'but I do want to help.' Her eyes lit up suddenly. 'I know—you have to take my twin, Cha Mina! She lives in Ik! How could I have forgotten? And she's just like me—a Readakin, loves to talk, brave as anything.'

'That's what I was afraid of,' muttered Tufan under his breath. 'Blahdeblah the Second.'

Zvala coughed loudly to stifle her giggles. 'At least,' insisted Cha Patti, sensing their resistance, 'she can give you a few lessons in tracking. That way, you will be able to follow whatever trail markers are still left.'

'Now you're talking!' said Zarpa. 'Sign us up for those lessons rightaway.'

The giant mithyaki looked as thrilled as a mithyatot who has just been given a giga-sized stick of rainbow cloud candy. 'And I'm going to pack you lots of slices of heat-and-eat Syntizza with all *kinds* of different toppings.'

'Awwww, thanks for everything, Cha Patti,' said Zvala, hugging her right leg hard. 'See you in an octoll!'

Eight

The Taranauts stared out of the windows of the black and silver snowbamba at the unchanging snowy landscape of Syntilla. Once in a while, another snowbamba would swish silently by, but apart from that, there was no life on the road. Sometimes they passed through strange silent forests of twisted needlecone trees, their dark green spikes black against the snow, and sometimes over creaky hump-backed bridges spanning dry canals through which the Bisibrooks had once flowed. Tufan sighed. How these canals must have looked then, chockful of plump, bright-eyed baby kurmoises splashing and playing happily in their warm depths!

Zvala looked away from the window and down at her All-Terrain Obverses, thinking that the silent Maraza had turned out to be quite a sweetie after all.

'Yes, it was really thoughtful of him to have got heatpads installed in them,' agreed Zarpa. "The boots were comfy enough, but what would we have done without our Obverses?"

Zvala looked up, startled. It was happening more and more now—they were all able to read each other's thoughts even when they were not stellipathing each other. It was great that they had all gotten so good at it, but then it wasn't so great either. She didn't *necessarily* want the others to know what she was thinking all the time!

'You'll have to work harder on your "erect fences, enclose thoughts" thingie then!' shrugged Tufan, grinning.

'Oh, stop it, you two!' said Zvala, beginning to turn a bright red.

'The Bell Trail!' announced the snowbamba driver mournfully.

The Taranauts tumbled out of the snowbamba with their bulging backsacks. Even before they had had a chance to thank their driver, the 'bamba had sped away, back towards the centre of Ik.

'On our own again,' sang Tufan. 'But,' he looked around, 'wasn't Cha Mina supposed to meet us here?'

'Yes, that's what Cha Patti said,' Zarpa scanned the trail, 'but we seem to be quite alone.'

Zvala gave a shout. 'There she is!' A figure in a grey snugsuit was hurrying towards them from further up the trail. As it came closer, they realized it wasn't a mithyaki at all, but a terrified-looking mithyaka. 'Trap at Cavity Crossing!' he panted, flinging a scroll at them and speeding away. Quickly, Zvala unrolled it.

'Hey, wait!' she said. 'This is a map of the trail, not a tracking guide. And it looks like it has been torn—' she pointed to the jagged edges, 'where's the rest of it?'

'Gone!' called the mithyaka over his shoulder. 'They took it!'

'Thanks, you've been a *big* help!' called Tufan, his voice loaded with sarcasm.

'Don't be mean, Tufan, can't you see he is terrified?' chided Zarpa. The three of them pored over the fragment.

'As far as I can tell,' said Zarpa, 'instead of just giving us a tracking lesson, Cha Mina bravely set out to walk part of the trail herself, maybe to check that the markers were in place, maybe even to plant markers where they weren't. She even made notes—for us—about the meaning of each

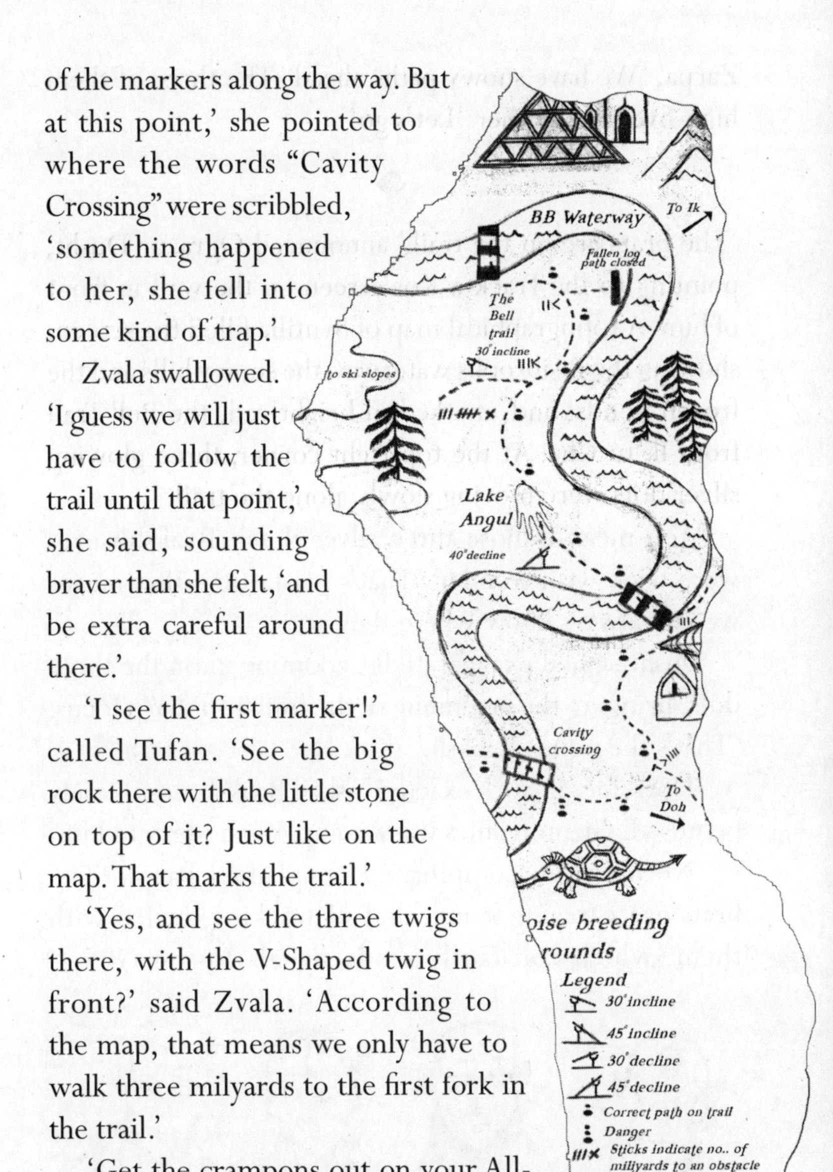

of the markers along the way. But at this point,' she pointed to where the words "Cavity Crossing" were scribbled, 'something happened to her, she fell into some kind of trap.'

Zvala swallowed. 'I guess we will just have to follow the trail until that point,' she said, sounding braver than she felt, 'and be extra careful around there.'

'I see the first marker!' called Tufan. 'See the big rock there with the little stone on top of it? Just like on the map. That marks the trail.'

'Yes, and see the three twigs there, with the V-Shaped twig in front?' said Zvala. 'According to the map, that means we only have to walk three milyards to the first fork in the trail.'

'Get the crampons out on your All-Terrain Obverses, team,' commanded

Zarpa, 'We have snowy paths ahead.' The three of them high-fived each other. 'Let's go!'

'The brats are on the trail,' announced Ograzur Dusht, pointing to the Track-a-Kos screen on the wall in front of him. A topographical map of Syntilla filled the screen, showing the Bisibrooks waterway, the snowy hills and the frozen ponds, and, marked in bright red, the Bell Trail from Ik to Cha. At the top right corner, three glowing silver dots were moving slowly along the trail.

'You mean—those three silver dots?' Raaksh's eyes were wide with wonder. 'That's mastastic—that means we will always know where they are!'

Dusht sighed exaggeratedly, zooming in on the three dots, bringing the beginning of the trail into sharp focus. 'That's the point, Raaksh.'

'How does it work exactly?' asked Raaksh, completely bemused. Gizmotronics was a complete mystery to him.

'Nothing too complicated,' explained Paapi. 'The brats are carrying some kind of tracking device with them, which constantly sends signals to the GPS—

Gizmotronic Personnel SearchSystem—here at Xad Yuntra. That's all.'

'And how exactly did we convince them to carry those devices?'

Shurpa smiled slyly. 'I bet they have no idea they are carrying them, bro. I bet it was Eye-in-the-Sky who slipped them into their backsacks when they weren't looking.'

The Ograzurs guffawed. 'Thank Kay Laas for Eye,' chuckled Raaksh. 'Good work, Dusht.'

'That was a very lucky break,' admitted Dusht, a condescending smile on his lips, 'and *most* unexpected. Dro Hie played a big part in it. Without her . . .'

'Don't you young ones *get* it?' cut in Hidim Bi, her face twisting in disgust. 'All this fancy gizmotronic mumbo-jumbo—the Track-a-Kos, the summoners—why, even the spies—are just aids! If the rest of you don't do what you are supposed to—and that includes *you*, Dusht!—a hazillion tracking devices won't stop the brats from rescuing the Silvers. And I assure you, the Master's anger if they do, will not be fun to watch.'

The Ograzurs stopped laughing. 'Raaksh, Shurpa, to your positions at the Crossing,' barked Dusht. 'If the brats do make it past that, you know what to do. Paapi, stay here and monitor the Track-a-Kos. Alert me the moment you notice something unusual.'

'Like what?' Paapi raised her eyebrows quizzically.

'Oh, use your brains! The dots could disappear. Or a dim fuzzy glow could appear, indicating the presence of another living creature. The device even detects body heat, so if you are watching *very* carefully,' he threw Paapi a pointed look, 'you will know someone's there even if he is not carrying a tracking device. Someone we definitely do not want could show up—like that weird mithyaka in the braid.' He gnashed his teeth. 'How I would *love* to get my hands on that guy!'

'Why *don't* you, then?' asked Paapi insolently. 'Or are you ashamed to admit that you have you no idea how to?'

'None of your business,' spat Dusht. He strode out of the room. The rest of the Ograzurs exchanged angry looks, but did as they were told. There was too much at stake now—and none of them wanted to return to the Fiery Lands.

'Okay, now what?' said Zvala. They were standing at the edge of Lake Angul. On the far side, the border of the lake wound in and out like a seaslith, creating long frozen 'fingers'. Around each finger hunched dense forests of gnarled needlecone trees. Narrow paths led off through the forests from each icy 'fingertip'. 'We know we have to cross the lake, but down which finger should we go?' Zvala wondered aloud. 'Everytime we go down a wrong finger, it will set us back by dings and dings!'

'Let's look at the map again,' said Zarpa, unscrolling the map. 'Hmm, it isn't very clear at all. I think we can rule out the end fingers, but it could be either of the fingers in the middle.'

'Pass me your durdekscope, Zarpa,' said Tufan, who had been thoughtfully and quietly scanning the landscape. 'Since the Syntillakos depend so much on trail markers to get around, I would imagine that they would have worked out something that can be seen from a *distance* in such situations.' He put the durdekscope to his eyes and zoomed in on the middle trails. After ten dinglings, he handed it back, sighing. 'Nothing. No twigs, no pile of stones, no message carved into the tree trunks, nothing.'

'Oh, I *wish* we were as tall as the Syntillakos,' groaned Zarpa. 'Then maybe we could have seen over the tops of the trees to . . .'

'Eeeeee! That's it!' yelled Zvala. 'We've been looking at the ground for clues, forgetting how tall the Syntillakos are! I bet Cha Mina left us a clue somewhere higher up! Tufan, can you check?'

Tufan lifted the durdekscope to his eyes again and gave a shout of triumph. 'I see it! The higher branches on the first two trees on either side of the left finger trail are all bent. It looks like they've been deliberately broken! That's our trail!'

'Yes, I see it too!' said Zvala. 'Even without the durdekscope—I'm sure that's the point.'

'Wait!' cautioned Zarpa. 'Those branches could have been broken anytime, by anyone. How can you be so sure?'

'Chillax, Captain!' said Tufan. 'They've been broken so recently that the sap is still oozing! Of course I can't be sure that it was Cha Mina who broke them, but someone or something tall went through there recently. It's our best chance!'

Zarpa shrugged. 'Set the Obverses to Glissade, then?'

'Yes,' said Tufan, bringing the aglets of his shoes together and touching the 'Glissade' icon. A thin sharp steel blade shot out from under each of his shoes, turning them into snazzy ice skates. 'Follow me!'

'Um . . . what . . . what if . . .,' stuttered Zvala, beginning to turn red.

'What *now*?' groaned Tufan. 'Don't tell me you've never skated before.'

'Actually, I was wondering if the ice was . . . was thick enough,' said Zvala, staring at the lake in fear. 'But . . . but yes . . . I've also never skated before . . .'

'Oh man! What did you *do* growing up apart from singing into your hairbrush and being supernerd?' snapped Tufan. 'Listen to me, Zvala! Do. Not. Freak. Out, okay? You know what will happen if you do, don't you? *You* will melt the ice and drown all of us!'

'Uh-oh!' said Zvala, getting redder still.

'Think of it as dancing, not skating,' suggested Zarpa, glaring at Tufan. 'Imagine you are on stage with Dana, and both of you are pirouetting and spinning and sliding like ballethak dancers. Imagine the crowds ooh-ing and aah-ing. Imagine all the starcasters of Mithya waiting to talk to you after your brilliant performance.' She paused, letting it sink in. 'Think you can, like, do that, girlfriend?'

Zvala smiled a small smile. '*To*-tally!' She bowed low to the cheering crowd, and stumble-stepped past the screaming paparazzi, gaining in confidence with each tiny glide. 'All interviews after the show, guys! Yes, yes, autographs too, I promise . . . .'

Nine

'I see Cavity Crossing,' called Tufan two dings later. 'Careful, now!'

The Taranauts walked gingerly up the path. Ahead of them, the ground dipped sharply into one of the channels of the Bisibrooks waterway. Once there had been a strong bridge across it, but all that was left of that bridge now were seven stout pillars, about a hazillion centinches apart, each coated with a thick layer of ice. They gleamed a cold silver in the light of the arcalamps, offering the only route across the now-dry waterway.

'They look like giant teeth to me,' shuddered Zvala.

'Wait,' said Tufan suddenly. 'Do you see what I see?'

The girls followed his gaze. 'What in Kay Laas are those?' said Zvala, her jaw dropping. On each of the last three pillars perched a large creature of some sort. Smooth meenmaachy heads with long snouts poked out of the front ends of the silvery semispherical shells on their backs, and twin-fluked tails flapped dispiritedly out of the other ends. Four clawed feet clutched on to the pillars for dear life.

'Silverbacked kurmoises!' whispered Tufan. 'Fine specimens, too—look at the beautiful shell colours and patterns! They look frozen nearly to death, the poor things. Starving too, I imagine. Come on, lets go to them.'

'*Wait*, Tufan! This could be the trap!' called Zarpa, but Tufan was already gone, leaping from pillar to pillar until there was just one pillar between him and the kurmoises. 'Come on, it's perfectly safe!' he called. Zvala and Zarpa waited for a moment, then shrugged and followed, taking their places on the first two pillars.

'I still think this is a bad idea,' began Zvala. 'How are we going to go any further now with the kurmoises blocking our way? I say we go back and rapseil down into the waterway . . .' she looked over her shoulder at the near bank and yelled in fright. The near bank had receded into the distance—there was no going back now!

'Muhahahahaha!' A shout of triumphant laughter cut her short. 'What did I tell you, sis? Was the kurmoise-in-distress setup a good idea or what? I knew that idiot boy would walk right into our trap!'

The Taranauts froze. On the other side of the waterway stood two vicious-looking Ograzurs, one male and the other female. 'Your second challenge, brats!' barked the female one. 'Getting to this side of the waterway. Only, there are two problems.'

She cleared her throat. 'Problem 1: the kurmoises. The *good* news is that you can jump from the back of one kurmoise to another and reach this side. The *bad* news is that if you jump on to a kurmoise back, you will shatter its brittle shell, causing it excruciating pain.' Her face twisted in delight.

'Problem 2: *the kurmoises*!' continued the male Ograzur, hooting at his own joke. 'The *good* news is that these are circus kurmoises, trained to leap great distances, so they can leap from one pillar of the bridge to the next one, or even the one after that, quite easily. The *bad* news is that they don't move at all unless they are instructed to—and the only voice they obey is their trainer's.' He looked around him. 'Hmm. I don' t see him around. Maybe, just *maybe*, it's because we have put him away somewhere?' He guffawed loudly.

'The next piece of your map is here,' said the female Ograzur, pointing to a fragment on the trail. 'If you ever get here, it will be waiting.' The male Ograzur hooted again. The next dingling, they had vanished.

'If either of you is thinking of jumping on the kurmoises' backs to get to the other side, be warned—you will have to fight me first,' Tufan said, his voice low and firm.

'Oooh, you scare me, strong guy!' Zvala made a face. 'As if we'd *dream* of doing such a thing! This sounds to me like one of Achalmun's problems—let me try and work it out. If the kurmoises and the three of us move correctly in sequence—us leaping over the kurmoises, they leaping over us—we should be able to do this.'

'We have to leap *over* the kurmoises?' Zarpa looked very worried, 'Will we be able to jump so far? I could stretch across, I suppose, like I did across Budbudana, but there is nothing to lock my feet around on either side.'

'No need for you to stretch,' said Tufan. 'If we use a combination of Hovitation and Kalarikwon, it shouldn't be too difficult for us to do it. And we have plenty of time.'

No, you don't! The Taranauts jumped. Someone had spoken right into their heads and it sounded very much like Cha Patti. *This is Cha Mina*, continued the voice. *I'm inside the pillar below the pretty girlkin.* Zvala allowed herself a pleased little toss of the head. *You've already been on the pillars eight dinglings.You have to cross in the next twenty-four,*

or the trapdoors at the tops of the pillars will open up and swallow you!

Thanks for that update, Cha Mina! stellipathed Zarpa. *Zvala, hurry!*

Her hands shaking, Zvala pulled out her scratchscribe and palmyra pad. 'I'm on the job,' she said.

'Tufan, talk to the kurmoises!' said Zarpa urgently. 'Never mind about the trainer—you know animals always listen to you.'

'I'll try my best,' promised Tufan. He pulled out his crittercaller, scrolled down the menu to 'Silverbacked Kurmoise', and blew gently into it. The kurmoises' heads came up in surprise. The creature two pillars away looked very like a mithyakin, but he squawked exactly like a kurmoise! 'You can trust me, boys,' whispered Tufan soothingly. 'Don't worry about anything now. I'll get you out of here real soon.'

'Got it!' yelled Zvala ten dinglings later, tearing out the page with the solution. 'I don't need this anymore—I've memorized it. Here, Tufan, you tell the kurmoises when to move, and I will tell Zarpa.' She threw the page into the air. Tufan inhaled hard. The page flew straight to him.

'Okay, so I make the first move!' said Tufan, studying the papyrus. He focused hard. 'Now!' He rose into the air, hovitating expertly, then executed a flying leap and landed on the central pillar. 'Your turn now, boy,' he cooed to the first kurmoise, pointing to the pillar behind him. 'Jump!' The kurmoise hesitated, squawking in alarm. Tufan bent into a crouch. He squawked and talked, and talked and squawked, his voice low and steady, urging it on. Finally, the kurmoise decided it could trust this strange but gentle creature. It hoisted itself onto its hind legs, and leaped.

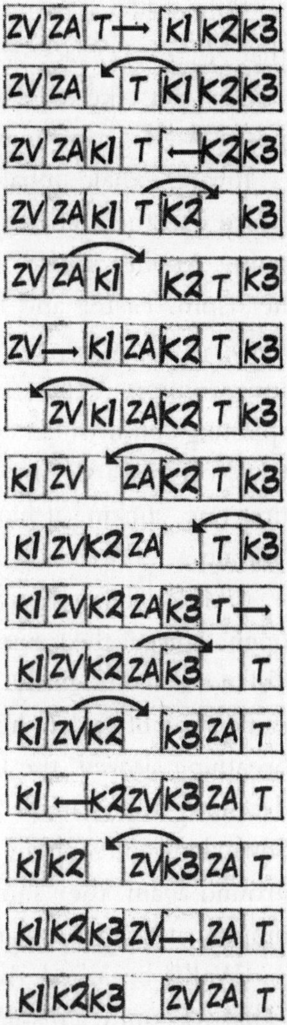

'Hurray!' yelled Zarpa and Zvala as it sailed over Tufan and landed neatly on the pillar behind him. *Hurray*! agreed Cha Mina, who had appointed herself cheerleader and timekeeper. *Eight dinglings to go*!

After the first kurmoise had leaped, the other two lost their fear. They had a trainer once again, someone who told them exactly what to do, and they were glad to obey. Just five dinglings later, Zvala and Tufan were high-fiving each other on the opposite bank.

Something was bothering Zarpa, though. She looked across to the kurmoises, and her face turned ashen. 'Guys, we made a big mistake. The kurmoises are still stuck. They can't leap to the other side—it has retreated even further away! And the trapdoors . . .'

'Oh, no! I was focusing so much on getting *us* to safety that . . .' Zvala's face crumpled with guilt.

'Let me take care of this,' said Tufan grimly, taking position—legs apart, arms akimbo.

Inhale, exhale, inhale, exhale. Tufan's chest began to heave like the seabed under Dariya as he got his lungs going. Mighty inhale. Headspin. Mighty exhale, rapid headspin. Faster and faster, faster and faster. With a *whooooosh*, the warm current of air spinning out of Tufan's lungs whipped the cold air around into a towering, spinning spiral. Tufan continued to exhale. The tornado took off towards the kurmoises. It zipped over the first one, sucking it high into the vacuum in its centre. Second . . . third . . .

CRASH! The seven trapdoors on top of the seven pillars opened just as the tornado picked up the third kurmoise. Tufan inhaled mightily. The tornado changed course and came straight back to him, carrying the kurmoises. As his breathing slowed, the tornado spun slower and slower, dropping the animals gently and safely on the snow. Squawking and scolding, but delighted to be back on solid ground again, they snuffled around the Taranauts' feet, nipping at their shoes and ankles.

'Well!' breathed Zvala, eyes round in admiration. 'That was quite a display! Well done!' Tufan bowed and sagged to the ground, exhausted. 'Although it would have saved everyone a lot of trouble,' she continued, eyes twinkling, 'if you had sucked up the kurmoises right at the beginning and dropped them on this side, *before* we did all the leaping around.' Tufan looked utterly chagrined.

'Sorry to play spoilsport once again, guys,' said Zarpa quietly, 'but aren't we forgetting someone?'

'Cha Mina!' Zvala slapped her forehead. 'We must rescue her!'

No, no, mithyakins! Don't worry about me! Someone will be along sooner or later . . .

No, Cha Mina. We are not leaving without getting you out of there, said Zvala firmly. *Now tell me, are you all the way at the bottom of the pillar?*

Yes, stellipathed Cha Mina. *Deep inside the cavity—can't climb out.*

Listen to me—crouch down inside. I am going to try and lop off about three-quarters of the pillar.

Okay, said Cha Mina. *I'm ready now.*

Zvala focused hard, repeating the Chant of Deep Stillness in her head. Then she sent a concentrated heat beam straight towards the point at which she wanted to cut down the pillar. The ice sizzled and smoked as it melted, revealing the stout wooden pillar beneath. Zvala kept the heat beam going. Slowly but surely, the beam cut through the thick hollow post. 'Timberrrrr!' yelled Tufan as the pillar keeled over and fell with a soft thud into a thick snowdrift. Silent wisps of smoke curled up from what was left standing. Nothing stirred.

'Cha Mina?' called Zvala, a worried edge to her voice. 'Are you okay?'

'Ta-da!' sang Cha Mina, as she emerged with a

grand flourish from inside the stump of the pillar. She looked exactly like Cha Patti. 'I've always wanted to do this, you know, like those actresses on starvision shows who emerge from birthiversary cakes and what not. Of course they're much prettier and everything, but tell me, very honestly—What did you think of my entrance?'

'You were fabulous, Cha Mina!' said Zarpa, smothering a grin. 'Wish we could stay and chat, but we've really got to be off. Will you be okay?'

'I'll be fine,' said Cha Mina. 'But will *you* three be okay? Are you sure you don't want me to come along with you, help you read your maps? And I can take care of you guys, you know, make you lots and lots of fudgebutter flipfloat, tuck you into your beds at night, read you bedtime stories . . .'

'No!' said all the Taranauts together. Cha Mina's face fell. 'But we'll be in constant touch—every time we can't figure out a trail marker, any time we need help.'

Cha Mina looked unconvinced. 'Promise?'

Tufan rolled his eyes at his companions. *Like we have a choice,* he stellipathed.

Cha Mina giggled. *That's right, you don't,* she stellipathed back, waving goodbye. *Stay safe, mithyakins. Big Mamma's reading you!*

Ten

'So the brats made it past Cavity Crossing,' fumed Dusht, staring at the three glowing dots on the Track-a-Kos screen, 'and are on the trail again!'

'Yes, but they wasted precious time rescuing the useless kurmoises,' chuckled Paapi. 'Bet they wouldn't have had they known just how useless they were. And now they have wasted even more time over that blabbermouth of a mithyaki. Pity—I would have loved to see her rot in there for a little longer.'

Dusht relaxed a little. 'Where are Raaksh and Shurpa?'

'There,' Paapi pointed to two red dots further up the trail. 'Waiting for the right opportunity. If all goes according to plan, they should be able to prevent the brats from getting to the Bridges of Setuway by fliptime.'

'Good,' said Dusht. He stared at the glowing dots, trying to tune into the Taranauts' thoughts. But there was only muffled static—the brats were getting better at fencing in their thoughts. He would need to make a bigger effort to read them, but there was no need for that right now. He turned to leave, and froze. He was receiving something! He closed his eyes, concentrating. It was a high musical voice, and he could hear it so clearly that the speaker might have been in the room with him. *That's right, you don't,* it giggled. *Stay safe, mithyakins. Big Mamma's reading you.*

Dusht opened his eyes, stunned. The voice was a Readakin's—he was certain of it! He would never have been able to hear her so easily otherwise. He hadn't known there were any left in Mithya with the ancient gift!

He recalled everything he knew about Readakins. For a good stellipath, Readakin thoughtwaves were notoriously easy to read. Many octons ago, the best stellipaths had been hired to find Readakins in exactly this way. Once they had been found, they had been hunted down and destroyed—mithyakos believed, mistakenly, that because they could hear mithyakin thoughts, Readakins were evil witchudails who would steal mithyakins' souls. After one such terrible round-up, the few remaining ones had gone underground, and had never been heard of again.

And yet, incredibly, here was a Readakin! He would just *have* to get her over to the Master's side. Then the brats would be entirely in his control. And if she did not cooperate? Dusht's mouth twisted in a half-smile. Like the Master said, there were many ways to skin a bekkat.

'Capture that mithyaki!' he barked, turning to Hidim Bi. 'You only have the octite!'

'Shush, you guys!' scolded Zvala, as she thawed and baked slices of frozen Syntizza between her hands. 'I can't hear myself think with all your squawking! And stop undoing my shoelaces already!' The kurmoises squawked even louder, their shells glinting dull silver-and-rainbow in the light of the faraway Tarasuns.

Tufan, who had just descended from the stilt-tent, freshly spritzed with Max Deo, grinned as he popped a delicious slice of hot Syntizza into his mouth whole. 'Deal with it, Firegirl,' he mumbled. 'We've been adopted! '

'Ewwwww,' Zvala screwed up her face. 'I don't *really* need to see the half-chewed contents of your mouth, you know! Bet *that's* why the Elders first came up with the idea for stellipathy—they must have known one of your ancestors, you . . . you . . . Malodorous Masticator!'

Tufan looked at Zarpa. 'Why does she use such big words always?' he asked, feeling Zvala's forehead with the back of his hand. 'I think the poor mithyakin suffers from a serious superiority complex.'

'So,' said Zarpa loudly and firmly, pinning Zvala with a look, 'on to Challenge 3! Now that we have the kurmoises, we don't need the map any more. These guys will be able to lead us down the trail. Right, Tufan?'

Tufan shook his head sadly. 'Small problem. Looks like these three were born and raised entirely in the circus. See how they have no fear of mithyakos at all? And it's clear they have *no* idea how to use their tracking skills, or they would have abandoned us and waddled off long ago.'

Zvala groaned. 'Uffpah! They will be wanting us to feed them next!'

'Uh-hunh,' agreed Tufan. 'They would have been fed all kinds of delicacies before the Depressiccate—meenmaach roe, muggar mottegs, maybe even fudgebutter flipfloat on very cold nights, but we will have to make do with barafberries for now.'

Zarpa shrugged. 'We'll make the best of it. Back to the map, then, guys,' she held up the second fragment of map. 'Just four octites to go to rescue the Silvers.'

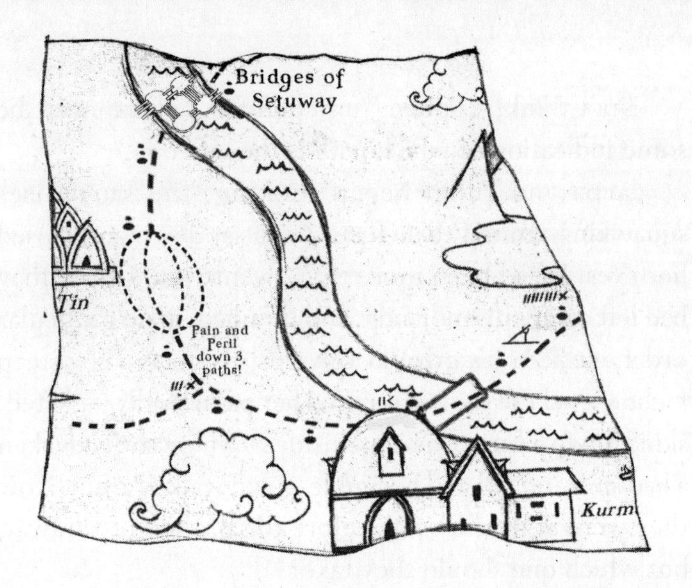

'So we have to first look for a marker like this,' said Zvala, pointing to the symbol of an inclined stick with another stick propping it up at its higher end.

'I see it,' said Tufan. 'What does it mean, though?'

Zvala pulled the first fragment out of her backsack and checked Cha Mina's notes. 'See, it's very similar to this one,' she pointed, 'and it means we have a steep descent ahead of us. Ungggghhh—I HATE descents.'

'Too bad,' snapped Zarpa. 'Start marching!'

'Another fork,' sighed Zvala. 'Four paths to choose from, and no markers anywhere.'

Zarpa looked at the map. 'All the paths seem to lead to the same place, but,' her voice trembled a little, 'it says here that some terrible danger awaits those who travel down three of them.'

'Let's think, Captain,' urged Tufan. 'There must be some indication of which path is the safe one.'

Zarpa and Tufan began looking, the kurmoises squawking around their feet. Zvala sat down and closed her eyes. It had been more than twenty dings since they had left camp this morning, and they had, in no particular order, walked milyards and milyards, clambered up a steep incline—where she had scraped her palms badly—skated, skied down a snowy mountainside—where she had taken a bad spill and twisted her ankle—and walked again. Now they were at the fork just before the Bridges of Setuway, but which one should they take?

'Nothing,' declared Tufan ten dinglings later. 'Nothing on the ground, nothing higher up, no clue whatsoever.'

'I know!' said Zarpa, lying down on her stomach and locking her feet around a needlecone tree. 'Let me stretch myself a little way down the paths, one by one. Maybe there are clues further down. That way, all of us don't have to tire ourselves out.' She threw Zvala a concerned glance and began to stretch down the first path.

The kurmoises watched her in silence for a few dinglings, then burst into a loud cacophony of alarmed squawking. They put their noses to the ground and began to waddle from path to path, sniffing the ground doubtfully.

'Nothing unusual down that one,' announced Zarpa, snapping back to her normal size a few dinglings later. 'Nothing good, but,' she sighed in relief, 'nothing bad either.' She looked at the squawking kurmoises curiously. 'What's with *them*?'

'Don't know,' Tufan shrugged. 'But it looks to me that they have suddenly realized that they have a higher purpose in life than undoing shoelaces. Maybe they will rediscover their natural tracking abilities!' He held up two crossed fingers.

'Going down the second one now,' said Zarpa, beginning to stretch. She slithered rapidly down the path, keeping her eyes peeled for any sign of danger, alternately scanning the ground and the trees above for any clue that would indicate this was the right path. She had reached the limit of her stretch when—

'Hey!'

Zarpa froze. A young smiling mithyaki in a high ponytail had suddenly appeared down the path.

'Ms Twon d'Ung!' Zarpa cried out in delight. 'What are you doing here? How . . . how . . .'

'I'm not actually here, my sweet galumpie,' said Twon d'Ung. 'This is just a holographic projection. I sensed that the Taranauts needed help, so 'I beamed myself here.'

'Wow! Thanks, Ms Twon d'Ung! It's so great to see you!'

'Ditto,' smiled Twon d'Ung. 'Now go back and bring the others. This is the safe path to the Bridges.' The next dingling, she had disappeared.

Back at the fork, one of the kurmoises, the smallest of the three, seemed to have come to a decision. Without consulting the others, he began waddling down Path 4 at great speed. Instantly, the other two set up another bout of agitated squawking. They would not go down the path themselves, but stood at the head of it, alternately scolding their truant companion and looking up at Tufan's face pleadingly. 'Oh, all right!' grumbled Tufan. 'I'll go and bring that sillykoof back.' He began to walk quickly down the trail.

'O-ho-ho, look who's here!'

Tufan stopped short, all senses alert. Then his face split into a ginormous grin as he caught sight of the merry-eyed mithyaka who had stepped out onto the path in front of him, a red-and-silver braid swinging down his back. 'Zub!' he cried. 'I *knew* we could count on you!'

Zub bowed elaborately. 'I try to please.' Squawking in fear, the kurmoise took cover behind Tufan, nipping his shoes.

'It's only Zub, boy,' Tufan reassured him. 'So Zub, this is the safe path, then?' Zub nodded. Tufan patted the kurmoise. 'Good job, boy—you found the right path! Come on, Zub, let's go tell the others!'

'Lead the way!' said Zub. The two of them started back up the path to the fork.

Back at the fork, Zvala slowly opened her eyes, yawned and stretched. Her little nap had done her a world of good—her brain felt ready to begin thinking again. She shushed the kurmoises, wondering where Zarpa and Tufan were.

'*Zvala, listen to me! There isn't much time!*' Zvala sat up with a start. '*Cha Mina?*'

'*Yes. Shaap Azur's goons are after me . . . can't run for much longer . . . but I just remembered something . . . thought it might help. The fork before the Bridges—only one of those paths is safe, the others are full of Downsiders . . . . Third from the left . . . got that? Third from the left . . . Uh-oh . . .*'

'Cha Mina?' Zvala called out aloud. 'Are you okay?' There was no answer.

Zarpa and Tufan burst out of Paths 2 and 4 at exactly the same time. Zvala waved them over excitedly. 'I know which one's the safe path!' they all yelled together.

Eleven

'It's Path 2!' said Zarpa. 'Ms Twon d'Ung said so!'

'No way!' said Tufan. 'It's Path 4. Ask Zub—he's never wrong!' But Zub had vanished.

'Cha Mina assured me it was Path 3,' said Zvala. 'And now she's been captured again—by Shaap Azur!'

'That doesn't smell right,' said Tufan. 'What would Shaap Azur want with Cha Mina? She doesn't even know us.'

'But she can *talk* to us, sillykoof!' retorted Zvala.

'And how would Shaap Azur know that?' returned Tufan. 'Like he has nothing better to do with his time than tune into the thoughtwaves of every citizen of Mithya!'

'What stinks to *me*,' said Zvala, changing the subject, 'is Zub! Why would he tell you which the safe path was, and then disappear? '

'Because that's what Zub *does*!' said Tufan. 'Plus, he has an excellent record—he has never given us bad advice.'

Zarpa cleared her throat. 'Pardon me for interrupting,' she said, eyes darting fire. 'But considering that among the three of us, only I had my information from an Achmentor, I think we should start walking down Path 2 now.'

The three of them faced each other belligerently, arms folded across their chests. Then Zarpa turned and began walking down Path 2. Zvala and Tufan exchanged quick glances. 'Zarpa!' they yelled, running after her. 'You can't do that! We're a *team*, remember? We'll play straight into Shaap Azur's hands if we don't behave like one.'

Zarpa stopped. 'There is something really strange going on,' continued Tufan, 'and if we don't put our heads together and figure things out, we're going to be in big trouble.' Zarpa's shoulders sagged. 'Guess you're right,' she said, beginning to walk back. 'Sorry.'

'All is forgiven,' said Zvala cheerfully. 'Now, did you actually *meet* Ms Twon d'Ung?'

'Um . . . not *quite*,' admitted Zarpa. 'It was a holographic projection. She said she had beamed herself down to help us.'

'Hmm . . . I don't like it,' said Zvala. 'None of our Achmentors has ever appeared on any of our rescue missions—why now?'

'And why appear only to you, and only when you were at full stretch?' said Tufan. 'It's almost as if she didn't want you to get any closer, because then you'd know she

was a fake.' He turned to Zarpa. 'Think hard—was there something she said or did that wasn't like her?'

Zarpa frowned, thinking hard. 'We-ell,' she said, flushing slightly. 'She called me her sweet galumpie, and she has never done that . . .'

'Sweet galumpie?' Zvala looked appalled. 'No Achmentor would ever address a student that way!' Tufan staggered around, clutching his throat and making gagging noises. 'Sweet galumpie!' he said hoarsely. 'And you *still* believed she was Ms Twon d'Ung?'

'Suppose you stopped dying for a dingling,' Zvala glared at Tufan, 'and thought about Zub a little? Are you really, really certain it was him?'

Tufan closed his eyes and thought back to his encounter on Path 4. He remembered his sudden fear, then his great delight as he recognized Zub, the merry twinkle in his eyes, the red-and-silver . . . . *Red-and-silver?* 'No!' he said grimly. 'It *wasn't* Zub after all! Unless . . . he has started threading his braid with red and silver instead of indigo and gold . . .' He paused. Then he shook his head. 'Naah, he wouldn't.'

'Red and silver?' said Zvala, in a perfect imitation of Tufan's tone. 'And you *still* believed he was Zub?'

'Oh, shush! all right,' snapped Tufan. 'I'm only wondering about the kurmoise.' He turned to look at the smallest kurmoise, and began to laugh. It had taken a short walk down Path 1 and was waddling back. 'He

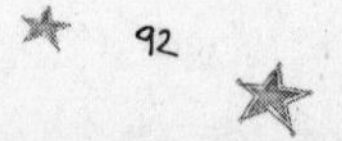

hasn't turned supertracker yet! He's just doing a little exploring down *every* path.'

'What about you, Zvala?' said Zarpa. 'Have *you* thought back to . . .'

'I have,' said Zvala, her face clouding with worry. 'And I'm certain it was Cha Mina, and that she has been captured. But . . . was she right about Path 3 being the safe one? I don't know! This part of the trail is quite a way from Ik, and I don't know how well she knows it . . . And what of Path I?'

Zarpa sighed despondently. 'Back to square one.'

'So,' said Tufan slowly. 'If it wasn't Ms Twon d'Ung or Zub that we met, who was it?'

'Morphoroops, I guess,' whispered Zvala, blanching. 'Remember when one of them entered the Tower Room, looking exactly like Ms Shuk Tee?' She stiffened suddenly. 'Wh-wh-what's that?'

Skrr-rr-rich, skrr-rr-rich. It was a small sound, and it sounded very like a kurmoise dragging its feet along the ground, but the Taranauts were taking no chances. They leapt to their feet and went into defensive positions.

Skrr-rr-rich, skrr-rr-rich. A smiley head poked out from between the lowest branches of the trees to their right. *Skrr-rr-rich, skrr-rr-rich.* The rest of the kurmoise began to emerge—forelegs, beautiful iridiscent midnite-blue shell patterned in dull gold—unusual for a silverback, double-fluked tail. The Taranauts relaxed. 'Where did *you* come from, boy?' said Tufan, bending down to scratch the kurmoise under the chin. 'You scared us.' The kurmoise squawked in alarm and tucked his head into his shell. 'Sorry, sorry,' whispered Tufan, hurriedly retreating a few paces. 'Forgot you're not used to mithyakos.'

The kurmoise slowly poked its head out again. Then it sniffed the ground, and unhesitatingly began to walk down Path 3. The three circus kurmoises followed, completely unafraid. Tufan looked at the others in triumph. 'Path 3—that's the safe one!'

'Morphoroop?' mouthed Zarpa.

'Negative. Our kurmoises would never have warmed to him otherwise. The little one reacted very badly to "Zub"'—Tufan shook his head in disgust. 'I should have realized he was a fake right then.'

'You can beat yourself up later—I'll help,' promised Zvala. 'But we'd better hurry now or we will lose our wild kurmoise!'

Hoisting their backsacks onto their shoulders, the Taranauts ran down Path 3.

Cha Mina sat on the uncomfortable chair in the damp cell, completely trussed up. Ograzur Dusht paced the floor in front of her like a caged shardula. She was tough to crack, this one, he thought, with her defiant eyes and her stubborn refusal to buckle. He had tried everything he could think of over the last 48 dings, but she, like all the other giant mithyakos of Syntilla, had an enormous tolerance to pain. He was frustrated now, close to exhaustion, and, he had to admit, desperate. The Master was going to want results soon.

Well, he would get them. If the mithyaki wouldn't come over nicely, they would just have to make her. Paapi was on her way to the cell right now, with the Manasbloer, the top-secret gizmotronic machine she was helping develop at Xad Yuntra. Once they wired the giantess up to it, all her thoughts, all her stellepathic messages—past, present and future—would become theirs whether she liked it or not. It was still untested, so no one was quite sure how long mithyakos could be wired up safely, but this was not the time to worry about that.

A sudden spasm of fear and guilt shot through Dusht. He hadn't expressly taken permission from the Master to try out the Manasbloer. The Master had his quirks, and one of them was his passion for gizmotronics. He had even set out the Ten Commandments of Gizmotronics for his staff to follow. One of them was about not using such devices on mithyakos until they had been properly tested and certified.

On the chair, Cha Mina realised she was running out of time. She had to do something quickly! She glanced at Dusht. He looked distracted, preoccupied. This was her chance to shut down her brain completely the way only Readakins could in times of danger. It was pretty drastic—her body would shut down too, except for its vital functions, as it entered the Zone of Anti-Consciousness, and the poor mithyakins would be all alone. If only she could get in touch with her twin before she shut down and tell her to take care of them! But how, *how*? If she stellipathed her, someone might intercept it. That would be catastrophic—Dusht would realize there was another Readakin on the loose and go after Cha Patti. She racked her brain—there must be some way . . .

Cha Mina sat up straighter as a sudden thought struck her. It was a memory, really, from her childhood, of her mother telling them about a special kind of natural stellipathy that only twins shared . . . what was it called now . . . oh yes, *Dilipathy*! It was a communication between hearts, not minds; a communication through feelings, not thoughts. And the best part, their mother had said, was that it was absolutely private—nothing and no one apart from the two of them could ever hope to listen in. She and Cha Patti had laughed about it—their mom told them so many fantastical stories that they never knew when she was telling the truth. But . . . maybe, just *maybe*, she had not been making this one up. It was certainly worth a try . . .

Twelve

'The Bridges of Setuway!' announced Zvala as the Taranauts emerged from the path and onto the bank of yet another branch of the Bisibrooks waterway. This branch was much wider than the others, too wide for a single bridge to span it. But there were islands in the middle—or at least they would have been islands when the Bisibrooks still flowed—connected to both banks and to each other by a series of short, sturdy-looking bridges. There was no need to stretch, hovitate, leap—easy-peasy protlee!

Zvala began to run towards one of the bridges. 'Wait!' called Zarpa, reading from an old, cracked sign by the side of the canal. 'There are some rules for crossing the bridges.'

'And look at this,' Tufan was studying the three stones piled on top of each other down the path to the bridges. 'According to Cha Mina's notes, it means . . . *danger.*'

Yes, it does. Follow the rules for crossing or the bridges will hurl you into the canal. You could have swum to safety if there was water there, but now, you will just get very badly hurt.

Cha Mina! cried Zvala happily. *You're okay!*

This is Cha Patti, said the voice, its tone subdued. *Cha Mina has been captured, but she is safe for now. She can't help you, though—she is in the Zone of Anti-Consciousness. I am now your only point of contact.*

The Taranauts exchanged fearful glances. *Thanks a hazillion for the update, Cha Patti*, said Zarpa. *We'll be in touch.* She paused. *And . . . and don't worry about Cha Mina. Once we've rescued the Silvers, we will rescue her. That's a promise.*

You're the best mithyakins. Cha Patti's voice shook.

Zvala turned back to the others. 'Now to crack the problem of the bridge crossing,' she said, pulling out a scratchscribe. 'Let's put it down on my pad first.'

'There is only a certain number of mithyakos that can cross a bridge—the numbers by each bridge indicate how many,' said Zarpa. 'Also, you can't cross in the same direction twice, or cross two bridges in a "set" at the same time.'

'I suppose we should count each kurmoise as equal to one mithyakos,' said Zvala. 'Oh, and are we taking all the kurmoises or just the wild one?'

'All of them, of course, Ms Selfish!' Tufan was scathing. 'And it isn't as if you even care about the wild kurmoise—you are only interested in him because he is useful! The wild one can manage perfectly well by himself—it is these three that need us!' He turned away in disgust.

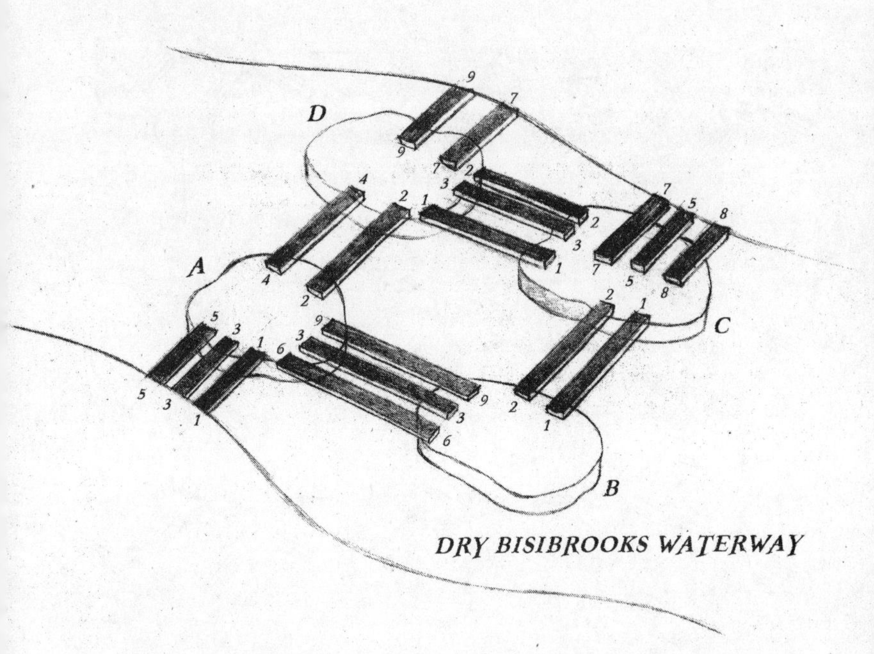

Zvala flushed, tears stinging her eyes. 'Hey, I was just asking, okay? To get a head count before I started solving the problem. I was always going to come back for them at the end of the octoll—there are enough barafberries here so I thought they'd be okay.'

'Whatever.' Tufan hunched his shoulders and walked off.

Zarpa put her arm around Zvala's shoulders. 'Seven of us in all,' she said. 'And eighteen bridges. Shouldn't be too difficult a problem for our brainiac.'

Throwing her a grateful smile, Zvala got to work, doing what she loved best—grappling with a problem that engaged her mind. Half a ding later, she gave a shout of triumph. 'Cracked it!'

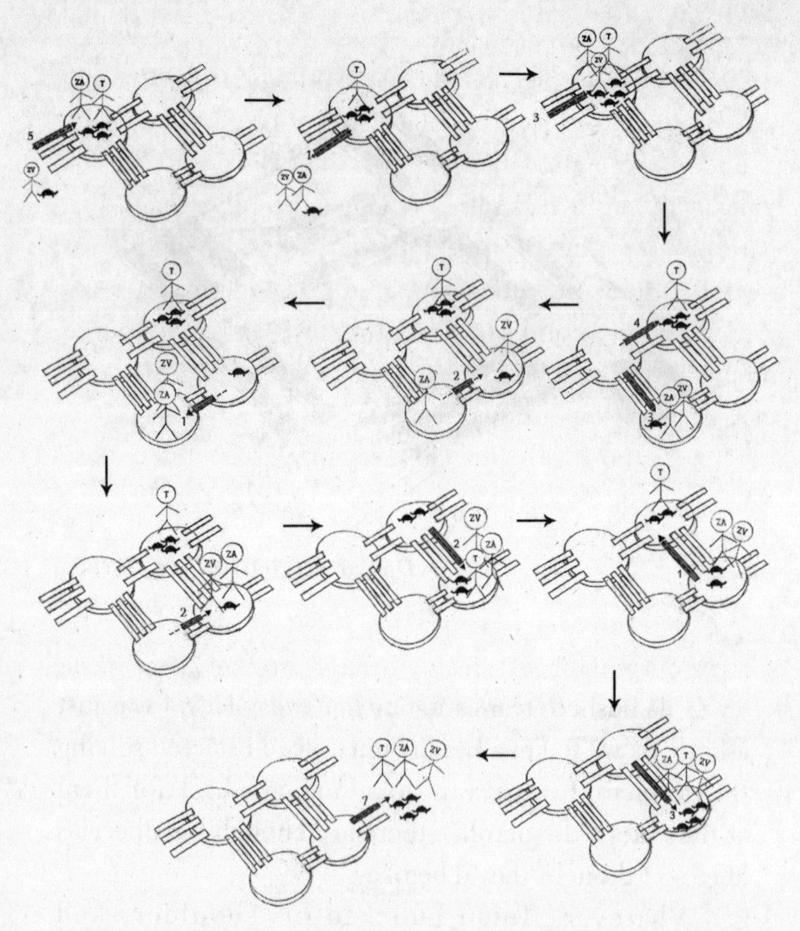

'Let me see!' Zarpa grabbed the pad. Interested despite himself, Tufan wandered over to peer over Zarpa's shoulder. Then he gave a long, low whistle. 'Mastastic!' he said admiringly. 'How do you *do* this stuff?'

Zvala shrugged. 'Maybe being selfish makes you good at puzzle-cracking,' she said in a small, tight voice. 'Come on, guys!' she called to the kurmoises. 'Who's going first?'

'There's another piece of the map!' yelled Zarpa, pointing to where a tattered bit of palmyra fluttered forlornly among the highest branches of a needlecone tree. The party of seven had safely reached the other bank just before fliptime the previous octite, and had quickly settled in for the nite. Now, after gorging on the last of their Syntizza and big bowls of mirchsicum-flavoured magginoo instachow, they were ready to set off again. 'Can you bring it down, Tufan?'

'Let's not waste time now on completely unnecessary things,' said Tufan. 'We only have 30 dings before our time runs out. We don't *need* a map anymore—the wild kurmoise will show us the way.'

'Of *course* we need it,' said Zvala, 'as back-up. The kurmoise might just decide to go his own way at some point. He's a wild animal, after all—and you can't predict when his "animal instincts" will take over.'

'Thanks for sharing your wisdom, Ms Zvala,' said Tufan, his voice dripping sarcasm. 'You are, of course, Mithya's acknowledged authority on animal behaviour.'

'Get the map, Tufan,' said Zarpa firmly. 'Zvala has a point.'

Tufan shrugged and raised his head towards the map, eyes flashing. He inhaled mightily, and the last piece of the map freed itself and floated down to them. Zarpa studied it. 'There's the Silver Bell!' she cried, pointing. 'Once

we're across this nameless lake here, we will be nearly at the end of the trail! Let's go!' She tucked the map into one of her pockets and set off down the trail again, following the kurmoises.

Ten dings later, they had reached the last fork in the path. The kurmoises set off confidently down the right fork, the three tame ones following the wild one. Zarpa stopped to check the map, and gave a shout. 'Stop!' she called to the kurmoises. 'That's the wrong way! We need to go towards the *other* lake. Tufan, stop them—the map shows a danger symbol.'

'Let me see,' Tufan walked over to look at the map. 'Hmm. It certainly looks as if they are going down the wrong way, but . . .'

'Maybe we should double-check with Cha Patti . . .,' began Zarpa doubtfully.

'The kurmoises are going towards Lake Shawksar Ovar,' cut in Zvala, 'which is the home of the deadly bijlimaach. Deadly, but only to mithyakos, who begin to lose consciousness at the first touch of the maach's ionergy-packed antennae. As they sink, the bijlimaach attack, stripping the flesh off from the toes up.' She paused. 'How*ever*,' she continued, slowly and deliberately, 'bijlimaach antennae have no effect on kurmoises. In fact,' she paused, 'bijlimaach ranks among a kurmoise's favourite foods. Which is why the wild one is heading straight for it.' She threw Tufan a triumphant glance and rolled up the map. 'I rest my case.'

'You didn't even know what a kurmoise *was* last octoll!' sputtered Tufan, infuriated that Zvala's theory about "animal instincts" had apparently been proved right.

'There is such a thing as a wikipad,' said Zvala smugly. 'And even selfish mithyakos can read.'

Zarpa held up her hand. 'Okay, that's it!' she snapped. 'You guys snipe at each other one more time and I'm quitting the team!' She glared at them. 'I mean it.'

Their faces black as thunder, but their mouths firmly shut, Zvala and Tufan set off down the left fork.

'It worked, sis!' Raaksh hissed gleefully. 'They got taken in by the tampered map! They are heading straight for Shawksar Ovar—and us!'

'This is the best chance we've had so far, Raaksh,' said Shurpa solemnly. 'If we do this right, we have a real chance of becoming the Master's top team.' She put her hands on his shoulders. 'Be careful now—do *not* bungle it.'

Raaksh shook her hands off in annoyance. 'I won't. I know *exactly* how important this is.'

'Here they come now,' whispered Shurpa.

"Glissade" again,' said Tufan, popping the ice skates out of his All-Terrain Obverse Nanos. 'First we get across this lake, then we make for the Bell at zipspeed. Don't forget we still have to figure out how to ring a broken bell.'

'Uffpah! I *had* forgotten!' groaned Zarpa. 'Hurry!'

They were almost at the middle of the lake when Zvala saw it. 'G . . .Guys!' she stuttered. 'Look out below!'

The others looked, and their faces went white. Just below their feet, beneath the frozen surface of the lake, swam a hazillion-strong shoal of malignant-looking bijlimaach, their antennae glowing bright with several centillion watvolts of ionergy!

'Zvala!' called Tufan urgently. 'Stay calm! Stay *very* calm! We can do this! We just have to quickly and carefully turn around and go back! The ice will hold, don't you worry!'

'Oh no, it won't!' called a harsh voice from the opposite bank. 'Not if we can help it!'

As the Taranauts watched, frozen with fear, two Ograzurs began to move slowly and menacingly towards the lake, swinging heavy clubs.

Tufan recovered first. 'They are going to strike the ice and crack it!' he yelled. 'We have to stop them! But how? I can't use my breath to blow them away—it will warm up the lake surface.'

'Stellikinesis!' commanded Zarpa. 'The clubs look too heavy for any one of us to do it alone, but maybe if we all try together . . . Right, Zvala? *Zvala? ZVALA!!!*'

'Wh . . .what?' mumbled Zvala. She looked completely disoriented.

'Look at me!' said Zarpa. 'Listen to me! See those swinging clubs? We've got to get them away from those two! If we don't, we will get ionergised by the bijlimaach and *we will drown*! Do you understand?' Zvala did not react. 'We have to try stellikinesis!' continued Zarpa, her voice beginning to shake. '*Team* stellikinesis! Zvala, *we cannot do it without you*!'

The message struck home. Zvala's eyes came back into focus. 'Let's do it, then,' she said quietly.

'The mithyaka's club first,' said Tufan.

The three of them stared at the club in the Ograzur's hand, willing it to move towards them. For what seemed like several dings, nothing changed. The Ograzur kept coming, swinging his club. Then, suddenly, it happened! The mithyaka was left clutching empty air, his face blank with incomprehension, as the club flew out of his hands and sped across the lake.

'Landing station: Left bank!' called Zarpa. Zvala and Tufan nodded. A dingling later, the heavy club came down with a thump on the soft snow on the left bank of the lake, far enough away from the Ograzurs to cause any more mischief.

'Now for the other one,' said Tufan. They turned as one to focus on the mithyaki's club.

'Uh-oh,' whispered Zarpa, terror leaching the colour from her face. 'Too late!'

The mithyaki had hurled her club high into the air. As they watched, paralyzed with fear, it began to spin downwards at incredible speed, finally landing on the icy surface of Shawksar Ovar with a resounding thud. *C-R-R-AACK!* the surface of the lake began to shatter. Hairline fissures zigzagged across the surface in every direction from the club's point of impact, until the lake was covered in a giant makdiboochi web of fine cracks.

Sensing that a hearty meal was only dinglings away, the bijlimaach began to tap, tap, tap impatiently at the under-surface of the ice closest to Zvala. 'Move, Zvala! Move!' criedTufan. But Zvala was rooted to the spot, transfixed by the grinning bijlimaach. The next instant, the creatures had broken through. The ice splintered into a mazillion little floes that began to drift apart rapidly. Their antennae glowing, their sharp little teeth at the ready, the bijlimaach converged malevolently around the Taranauts as they plunged, limbs flailing, into the freezing water!

Thirteen

'Your Starness,' cried Cha Patti, bursting into the Maraza's chamber. 'The Taranauts are in trouble somewhere near Shawksar Ovar! I can't read them anymore, which means they have lost consciousness. Maybe because,' she gulped, 'the bijlimaach have got them.'

'Cha Patti!' Tin Patti rushed in behind her.' Stop your blabbering! You can't just barge into the Maraza's private chambers this way . . . .'

The Maraza raised an imperious hand. 'Let her speak.'

Cha Patti goggled. 'You speak!'

'Only when absolutely necessary,' said the Maraza. 'What do you mean, you cannot read them?'

Cha Patti flushed. 'I . . . I am a Readakin,' she said. Tin Patti looked aghast. The Maraza's expression did not

change. But he walked over to Cha Patti and shook her hand silently. 'An honour,' he said shortly. Cha Patti bowed, ecstatic. 'Now, what do you suggest we do?'

'We should go to them immediately,' she said simply. 'I know the trail well—we can go up the trail from Cha, instead of Ik. ' Her face clouded over. 'But it will take time, and I don't know if we have time . . .'

'Tin Patti,' commanded the Maraza. 'Get the troops together. We will stelliport to Shawksar Ovar.'

'Stelliport?' said Cha Patti. 'What's *that*, Maraza?'

'A trick I learnt in my years at Zum Skar,' smiled the Maraza. 'You will find out more soon enough.'

He was falling, falling, falling. It was so cold in the water, so dark. He was numb, senseless. But he could still see, still hear. He saw the bijlimaach around him, heard their jaws snapping. He saw the glowing red points of their antennae coming at him, for him. He should blow a bubble of some kind, he thought, enclose himself and the others in it. He should find *the others—where* were *they?*

But it was too much work, and his frozen muscles just wouldn't listen . . . Ouch! *The skin of his left cheek tingled hotly. Oh, well, the bijlimaach had got him.* Ouch! *Another one. And another.*

He couldn't focus anymore, couldn't think. It was almost a relief. Just before his eyes closed, he saw a flash of midnite blue and dull gold zip past him, followed in quick succession by three flashes of silver. The bijlimaach began to scatter. Tufan smiled. The kurmoises had returned.

'Tuuu-faaaan! Tuuuu-faaaan!' He was at the bottom of a deep well, and someone was calling down at him. *Oh, go away*, he thought irritably, I'm soooo sleepy. 'Tuuu-faaan! Wake uhhhp! It's just one diiiiing to fliiiptiiiime!' *And so?* he snapped. *So what?*

'The Bell! The Cracked Bell! The Silvehhhrs!' Tufan stirred. The Cracked Bell. The Silvers. It meant something, he was sure of it, something important. But he couldn't for the life of him remember what it was.

Fsssssst! What was that sound? It was very familiar. *Fssssst!* There it was again! Now he could even smell something. Something strong and sharp and limbulimey . . . Tufan opened his eyes.

'*Told* you that would do the trick!' Zvala was saying through a fog, waving a can of Max deo around like a banner of victory.

A crowd of Syntillakos were gathered around him—Cha Patti was there, he noticed, as his vision cleared, and Tin Patti, and was that . . . the Maraza? He could hear the kurmoises' muffled squawking in the distance. Zarpa bent concernedly over him. 'Are you okay? Can you see me? Do you know who I am?'

Tufan's face went limp. His voice shook. 'Dada,' he said. 'I knew you'd come to get me.'

Zarpa went white. 'He's hallucinating!' Zvala hurried over, biting her lip and trying not to cry. She and Zarpa had got away with just one bijlimaach sting each, and had recovered fully within half a ding of the kurmoises dragging them out of the water, but Tufan had been stung six times! She had been so happy that the trick with the deo had worked, but it looked as if Tufan's memory had been scrambled. 'He will know me!' she said, smiling sweetly at him. ' Recognize me, Tufan? Zvala?'

Tufan raised his hand weakly and beckoned to her. 'He wants to tell me something!' whispered Zvala, as she bent over to listen. 'Told . . .,' whispered Tufan. His shoulders sagged and his eyes closed again. 'Told who?' said Zvala, blinking back tears. 'Told Zvala? *What* was it you told someone?'

Tufan opened his eyes. Zvala nodded encouragingly and bent over him again. 'Told you we should have taken the right fork,' said Tufan clearly.

Zvala's head came up like a shot. Tufan lay there, grinning up at her. Zvala's eyes blazed. 'Well, of all the . . .' she said furiously, throwing the can of deo at Tufan. 'You know what? You should have just stayed there, at the bottom of Shawksar Ovar.'

Standing on top of the last hill on the trail, the Taranauts stared at the ginormous silver bell. It hung, silent and caked in ice, from a massive wooden frame that straddled the source of the now-dry Bisibrooks waterway. Less than half a ding to go to fliptime, and they hadn't the faintest clue yet how to get it to ring.

A crowd of Syntillakos waited at the bottom of the hill, too scared to come any closer to the 'haunted' bell. The wild kurmoise had wandered off into the needlecones after leading the rescue, and hadn't been seen since, but the three silver ones waddled around them, squawking peacefully. Cha Patti, after Zvala had assured her that they would be fine, *really*, had left to help with the rescue of Cha Mina, thrilled that the Maraza of Syntilla was personally leading the effort. Only Tin Patti stood on the hill with them, dour and silent, keeping a close watch for interlopers.

'The Syntillakos say,' said Zvala, gazing up at the humungous bell clapper that hung down above their heads, 'that the bell used to chime entirely on its own, twice a Taraday, as regular as anything. Eight gongs at fliptime, and eight again at 1 o'ding, when the Upside

emerged to welcome a new day with the Silvers.'

'Which means,' said Zarpa, 'that there is no point looking for a bell pull or anything like that.'

'Which also means,' said Tufan slowly, 'that it could be a gizmotronic bell, programmed to ring at particular times of the Taraday. And if that were true, there should be some kind of mechanism somewhere that makes it happen. If I were the one designing the bell, I would put it inside the post, somewhere accessible, easy to reach.'

'That makes sense,' said Zarpa. 'But remember—these are tall guys here.'

'Right,' said Tufan. 'Let's try and find the mechanism now—quickly! We're running out of . . . Heyyyyyy!' He cried out in alarm as he was suddenly lifted straight off the ground!

Zvala hooted. 'It's only Tin Patti!' she called to him. 'He has found the mechanism!'

'Hurry, Tufan!' called Zarpa. 'Twenty dinglings to go!

Perched on Tin Patti's shoulders, Tufan opened the little wooden door high up on the post that concealed the bell ringing mechanism. There was a mass of cuprowires inside, some broken, some bent. This was clearly the problem, but how in Kay Laas was he going to repair it without a circuitogram of some kind?

Circuitogram. The word triggered a memory. Where had he seen a circuitogram recently? He racked his brains. Somewhere, *some*where . . . He had seen it lying against the ice—lying . . . or *hanging*. A vision of the Ice Palace swam into his head—beds made of ice, ionergised blankets, rugs on the floor and hanging on the . . . That was it! The burning rug—it had turned into a circuitogram! A shiver of excitement ran down his spine. He could *bet* it was the circuitogram he needed.

'Put me down!' he yelled excitedly. As he rooted through his backsack, everything in it came flying out, including a small round disc that flashed silver in the snow. 'Found it!' His hands shaking, Tufan unscrolled the rug and studied it intently for a few dinglings. 'Pick me up again, please, Tin Patti,' he said at last. 'I know how to fix the bell.'

Tufan began to work feverishly. Ten dinglings to go.

Tin Patti cleared his throat. Zvala looked at him quizzically. 'You want to say something?' she asked. Tin Patti looked very embarrassed to be the one starting a conversation, but went ahead anyway. 'Um . . .,' he said, pointing to the silver disc that had come out of Tufan's backsack. 'What's that?'

'We have no idea,' shrugged Zarpa. 'One of our Achmentors gave it to us—said it would come in handy.'

Tin Patti looked even more embarrassed. 'What?' demanded Zvala. 'Do *you* know what they are?'

The giant mithyaka nodded slowly. 'Tracking devices,' he said. 'For spying. The Emperaza outlawed them many octons ago.'

Zvala and Zarpa stared at each other, stunned. That was how the Downsiders had always seemed to know where they were, how they had always stayed one step ahead of the Taranauts! In one smooth motion, they had upturned their backsacks and found the other two discs. Quivering with anger, they stamped on the discs again and again, warping them beyond repair.

Then another thought struck them both, simultaneously, like a thunderbolt. *They knew, without a doubt, who the spy in Zum Skar was*!

'Done!' From the top of Tin Patti's shoulders, Tufan waved to them. 'How many dinglings to fliptime?'

Zarpa glanced at her dingdial and held up two fingers. 'If I've done things right,' said Tufan nervously, 'the bell should ring out in two dinglings precisely.'

Zarpa and Zvala held hands tightly and stared fixedly at the dingdial. The crowd of Syntillakos fell silent. Tin Patti looked into the distance, not meeting their eyes. Tufan paced around the bell post, never taking his gaze off the clapper.

Fliptime! The light of the distant Tarasuns faded as Syntilla began to flip into Dariya. The Dar-Proofs began to slide silently up. More arcalamps came on. The Taranauts held their breaths.

BONG! BONG! BONG!

A joyful roar erupted from the bottom of the hill as four shimmering stars, blazing trails of shining silver, soared into the sky. Only the briefest glimpse, before Syntilla flipped completely, turning away from Tara for the nite. The Syntillakos would have to wait sixteen more dings, until Taralite, before they could fully enjoy the Silvers again. But no one was complaining.

On the hill, Tin Patti bent, making as if to sweep Tufan off his feet again, then thought better of it and patted his back awkwardly. Zarpa and Zvala threw their arms around each other, then ran to Tufan and hugged him hard. 'Yuckthoo!' he yelled, beating them off. 'Let go of me!'

BONG! BONG! BONG!

The hill began to thrum under their feet as something big and powerful moved underground. The crowd fell silent again, their faces taut with fear. The Taranauts clutched each other.

Something dark and viscous was leaking out into the canal below the bell. The liquid swirled and eddied. Bubbles rose slowly to the surface of the sludge and popped stickily, filling the air with the stench of rotten mottegs.

BONG! BONNNNNNG!

With a triumphant *WHOOSH!* a milyard-high fountain of silver spume shot through the sludge and into the air. In its wake came a mazillion tols of gurgling, laughing water. It gushed into the canal and danced joyously down the hill, spraying the Syntillakos on its banks and making them squeal with excitement.

Tin Patti turned to the Taranauts, his eyes bright with tears. 'The water—it's *warm,*' he said. 'You mithyakins . . . you have brought the Bisibrooks back.'

Zvala smiled and nodded. Then she turned away—she could not bear to see a grown mithyaka cry. All along the canal, the usually reserved Syntillakos were going completely crazy—whooping, laughing, chattering, and leaping into the water, snugsuits and all. One of them turned and saw her, and yelled something out to the crowd. The next instant, hazillions of Syntillakos were racing up the hill, screaming their' names. 'Uh-oh,' said Zvala.

'Uh-oh is right,' agreed Tufan. 'We have to get out of here quick! But how?'

'Where there's a will, there's a way,' said a merry voice. 'And where there's a *bell,* apparently, there's a *water*way!'

A blue and silver aquauto had appeared on the melting snow next to them. The driver's braid was threaded through with indigo and gold.

'Zub!' yelled Tufan in delight, leaping into the aquauto. Zarpa and Zvala jumped in behind him. 'You're a lifesaver!'

The aquauto, blaring Lustr Blasters Top Hits, plunged into the canal, away from the cheering Syntillakos. The kurmoises leaped in after it, squawking their heads off.

'No LB, *puh-leese* pretty please?' begged Zvala. 'I want to listen to the song of the water.'

Tufan sighed exaggeratedly, then leaned over and turned off the music. '*Just* this once,' he said. 'And you owe me. Bigtime.'

Zvala stuck her tongue out at him. He waggled his ears at her. Zarpa and Zub laughed. The aquauto sailed down the canal, rocking happily from side to side.

Fourteen

'I got you here to Zum Skar to give you the biggest break of your career,' Achmentor Twon d'Ung was angrier than anyone had ever seen her. 'And *this* is how you use it? Why, Aaq, *why*?'

Tufan had been wondering the same thing. He waited to hear what Aaq would say. Zvala and Zarpa waited, too.

'The former Marani of Glo,' Aaq's face was impassive, 'is my long-lost little sister. The one who disappeared all those octons ago.' Twon d'Ung looked stunned. 'I didn't know it when I first came here—she only got in touch two octolls later. It was the best news I had ever had in my life. So when she asked me to send her three summoners from the store here—urgent, no time for getting all the permissions—I did. Why would I refuse?'

'I can understand that—*some*what,' said Twon d'Ung, 'you may not have known what she wanted them for. But,' her voice hardened, 'what about *this* time? You *knew* whose side she was on. You *knew* that tracking devices were illegal . . . I guessed you were up to something, Aaq. I was so worried. I tried my best to tell you, in so many ways. But you wouldn't listen, would you?'

'She is my sister,' said Aaq simply. 'And she is in prison. One way to get her out was to help her side win.'

Twon d'Ung's eyes filled with pain. 'I always treated you like my little brother,' she said. 'Taught you right from wrong, looked out for you always. I would not have minded so much if you had only got yourself into trouble with your criminal ways, but you plotted against the Emperaza himself. Worse, you broke the Achmentor's sacred trust, Aaq. You put your students in danger,

terrible danger. And for that, neither Mithya nor I can ever forgive you.' Her face twisted in disgust. 'Get away from me, Aaq, I never want to set eyes on you again.' She turned and walked out of the room.

A shadow passed across Aaq's face. For an instant, the cool , arrogant Achmentor disappeared. He looked confused and hurt, like a mithyakin whose mother had abandoned him. Tufan's heart lurched. What if he had been in a similar situation, and Dada had asked him to do something for him? Something that he knew was illegal? Might he not have done the same as Aaq? Just to make sure Dada was free again? He didn't know. Achmentor Dummaraz was right—love was a very powerful thing.

'I heard about how you fixed the bell,' Aaq said suddenly, nodding at Tufan. 'It wasn't an easy circuitogram you had to work with there, and you had very little time. Great work—you have a brilliant future in gizmotronics.' Tufan flushed with happiness. 'MISTRI is ready—and tested,' continued Aaq. 'I have left the apparatus in your room. I didn't have the chance to enjoy it fully myself, but I'm happy that you will.' He was silent for a dingling. Then he looked straight at the Taranauts. 'I didn't really want any of you to get hurt, you know.'

'If you will kindly accompany us, sir.' Two stern-looking officers from Mithsafety had appeared at the door. Without another word, Aaq turned and followed them out.

There was a long silence, as the Taranauts wrestled with their own feelings about the whole affair. Zarpa glanced at Tufan. He looked devastated.

'So,' she said brightly. 'Suppose you explain to me how the Bisibrooks started flowing again?'

'It was the *sound* of the bell, wasn't it, Tufan?' Zvala picked up the cue. 'Remember how the Great Depressiccate happened after the bell "cracked"? The Syntillakos thought the evil spirit in the bell caused the Depressiccate and in a sense, they were right.'

'Yes,' said Tufan. 'The problem with the Bisibrooks is that black, sticky mud keeps blocking up the source of the water. So, many octons ago, some very clever Biggabheja designed the Silver Bell of Syntilla. The vibrations it set off when it pealed were strong enough to dislodge the mud, allowing the water to keep flowing. When the bell cracked, the Bisibrooks dried up!'

'Hmmm,' said Zvala, '*there's* an idea! Wonder if there is a way to permanently *block* holes instead of unblocking them, though . . .'

'That's always way easier,' began Tufan animatedly. 'For instance . . .' Then he noticed Zvala's twinkling eyes and stopped, looking at her suspiciously. 'Just *which* holes were you thinking of blocking?'

'The holes on a certain can of noxious deo, my stinky galumpie,' said Zvala, shrieking with laughter as she raced out of the room, with Tufan in hot pursuit.

'Someone *had* to have delivered your sister's messages to you, Aaq,' Shuk Tee's face was grim. 'She has no access to summoners or any messaging devices in her cell, and the anti-stellipathy shields around the cell have not been penetrated. Who was it? '

Aaq shrugged. 'You have to believe me—I don't know. The operation was very low-giz and primitive—the messages were always written on palmyra scrolls, and they were slipped under my door or placed on my worktable when I wasn't in the room.'

Shuk Tee considered. Aaq sounded like he was telling the truth. She gestured to the officers to take him away, and walked wearily to the window of the Tower Room. Whoever had slipped the messages to Aaq had to be the same person who had weakened the safety shield and allowed the Morphoroop in. Another octoll, another traitor. Would they *never* stop coming?